D0887119

HIGH NOTE, LOW NOTE

WESTMINSTER BOOKS BY ANNE EMERY

HIGH
NOTE,
LOW
NOTE

by Anne Emery

Philadelphia
THE WESTMINSTER PRESS

Library of Congress Catalogue Card Number: 54–5273

PRINTED IN THE UNITED STATES OF AMERICA

HIGH NOTE, LOW NOTE

THE minute Jean Burnaby entered her home room on the first day of school in her senior year, she was aware of a new personality in the group.

The new girl was sitting in the last seat across from the door, reading the Sherwood High School students' manual. But she glanced up as Jean stood in the door, and Jean knew she had looked swiftly and analytically at each newcomer in turn.

Now she smiled at Jean, and raised one finely curved eyebrow, as if to say: "Well, hello! You're the one I've been waiting for!"

Jean smiled back, noticing at the same time that all the seats around the new girl were filled. With a wave of her hand, she greeted the students she had known before and sat down near the front, next to Jeff Sutton.

"Hi!" Jeff laid down his program and turned toward Jean with a grin.

"Here we are again," said Jean, thinking how attractive Jeff looked after their summer apart.

About her the room hummed and chattered with reminiscences of summer: "We went up to Canada, and, boy,

7

you ought to see the fish up there! " " I had a job at the candy factory. Made $600, and coulda made more, only my folks said that's enough for one year." " Summer school was hideous, but I pulled my math grade up to a B." " I spent all summer reviewing for those college board exams this year."

Senior year. The year of college board examinations, of college plans, of scholarship applications. The last chance to improve her high school standing, the last chance to earn recognition at Sherwood High School, the last year she would be with these classmates. And Jeff —

Jean looked across and smiled at him again.

Slim and of medium height, with a wide smile, he had a subtle charm, a puckish humor behind his glasses, that Jean felt she enjoyed more than anyone else. Without exerting any noticeable personality, he seemed to contribute to the student body a quiet leadership that had earned him a great deal of respect in the two years she had known him.

She had gone with him since sophomore year. During her junior year they had quarreled violently over her sorority membership, and he had ignored her for several months. In spite of her sorority and going steady with a prominent senior, she had missed Jeff sadly, and recognized for the first time how much he meant to her. She had liked his company so much; he was so dependable in the ways that counted: he was not sentimental, he was a good dancer, they had so many things to talk about, and they laughed at the same things. When they had made up their quarrel in the last week of school, she had felt as if her junior year had been retrieved from disaster.

He had spent most of the summer as counselor in a boys'

camp, and had gotten home only the week end before school opened, when he had called her to let her know he was back, that he would see her this morning, and how about a date next Saturday night.

"Have you seen the new girl?" she whispered under the conversational din.

"How could I help it?" Jeff grinned mischievously. "Her name is Kim Ballard. Father is *the* J. Lloyd Ballard who wrote the Berlin dispatches for the *Tribune* last year. Anything else you want to know?"

"I knew I could count on you to give me the news," Jean said. "She looks interesting, don't you think?"

"Quite," said Jeff, with an emphasis she could not interpret. "Isn't that horsetail new? When I saw you last June your hair was short."

"Do you like it?" Jean switched her head a little, knowing that her hair was caught up at an angle becoming to her slim, piquant face, and that the red ribbon tied around it with a small bow and long ends was a new idea. "It wan't really short last June — I'd been working on this idea for a long time. It was down to here, then — " she measured close to her shoulders, "but I kept it curled so it looked shorter."

Jeff kept looking at her judiciously. "Yep," he said finally, "it looks good. But you can get away with the darnedest things."

He looked baffled as he returned to his schedule, and Jean, suppressing a giggle, picked up the papers before her. The teacher called her name and handed her a class schedule. Running her eyes over it, she remembered that she and Jeff had talked last June about the classes they wanted to take together. But that was before she had decided to take orchestra this year.

During the summer her piano teacher had fired a new spark, and music, at long last, had become very important. Jean had studied for years without any definite goal, and last year her sorority activity had thrust her practicing into the background, where she had maintained the minimum with effort. But between her junior and senior years she had realized, as she practiced the three hours a day her teacher demanded now, that she wanted to play really well, and that she would enjoy working with music more than anything else. Just before school had opened she had changed her course to include the orchestra, and she had not yet had a chance to tell Jeff about the change.

It was going to interfere with some of the classes they had planned to take together, and she hoped he wouldn't mind too much. Running her eyes over her other classes, she thought again of Kim Ballard, and wondered whether they would be in any classes together.

She turned around and looked again at Kim over her shoulder. Kim met her eyes and smiled. She was strikingly attractive, with short curly chestnut hair, hazel eyes, a pert nose. She was friendly, chic, self-assured. And a deep, audacious dimple made her smile daring and challenging, as if she were saying, " So you think I can't do it? " A tantalizing, daring, gay assurance curved her wide mouth irresistibly and sparkled wickedly in her eyes. Jean had a conviction that knowing Kim would be a dramatic adventure.

There was no chance to become acquainted that first period. When the bell rang, the class moved into the hall together, Kim with two boys and Jean with Jeff, and Jean did not see her again until fourth period, when they found themselves in the same study period. At that time Kim waved in recognition, and when they left the room at the end of the period Jean said to her: "You're new here, aren't you? I saw you in home room. Are you going that way now?"

Together they walked through the hall toward their lockers.

"My father graduated from Sherwood High School twenty-five years ago," said Kim, "and he wanted me to have a year here before I finished high school. We were abroad during my first three years."

Her voice was low, and she spoke with a faint difference of inflection — not so much an accent as a result of having heard other voices than American ones for a long time. Jean was captivated.

"You must speak foreign languages then," she said. "Did I hear that you'd been in Berlin?"

"Last year in Berlin, and two years before that in Paris," Kim said, with no suggestion of importance. "I learned French and German. Europe was fun, of course. But I'm terribly excited about America."

She smiled with that flashing suggestion of finding adventure wherever she looked, and of inviting Jean to share it with her.

"What are you taking?"

"History," said Kim. "Dad said I ought to learn American history in American terms. And English literature. Chemistry, because it seems to be required. And orchestra. I never had a chance to play with an orchestra before."

"What do you play?"

"I studied violin in Paris and voice in Berlin," Kim said. Jean knew that this girl would be good.

"I'm in the orchestra myself this year," Jean said. "I'm playing piano — and probably percussion instruments in between. I did some accompanying last year, and it was so much fun that this year I'm doing it for credit. Sometimes I think I may go on to music school, but I haven't decided yet."

"What I really want to do," Kim confided, "is to go on the stage. I've been doing some modeling for a friend of Dad's in the Loop — a photographer — " The name she mentioned was nationally famous, and Jean stared at her, speechless. "He says I shouldn't have any trouble being a model. But I'd rather act. A friend of mine is in the cast of *Seventeen* in New York. Did you ever hear of Nick Trumbull?"

Jean shook her head. "I'm not very much up on New York shows," she said apologetically.

Kim didn't seem to mind. "You might not have heard of him anyway," she said, opening her locker with a bang. "He's new in the cast. But he's very good. They're coming to Chicago this winter, and he's going to look me up."

"Come on and eat with me," said Jean, as they closed lockers and turned toward the cafeteria. She was fascinated with the glimpses Kim gave her so casually of a world she had never known, and her first reaction to Kim was confirmed: knowing her would be a dramatic adventure. She looked forward now to her orchestra period with more anticipation than before.

She found, when she arrived at the music room, that she knew several of the orchestra members by sight. Six of the boys had a dance band that had played for school parties; another dozen of the boys and girls were members of the Musicians' Club, which Jean had begun attending at the end of last year. One of the trumpets was in her history class; the first French horn was in her English class; Bonnie Richardson, sitting in the first chair in the violin section, had been in her French class since sophomore year.

Mr. Friedman, the director, rapped for order, and seventy-five musicians took their chairs and faced him. Jean and Kim sat together at one side, waiting for assignment. Mr. Friedman turned to Jean. He was short and stocky, with dark hair and eyes and a warm smile.

"So we have a new pianist this year?" he said. "I wondered if we should have one at all, since Grace graduated last year. You can play the triangle and the kettledrums when there is no piano part. And you're a violinist?" he looked at Kim. "Fine. Our string section is small. Will you sit with the first section, please. We'll try out for positions in about a month."

Jean moved back to the kettledrums, which she loved, and Kim took a chair at the back of the first violin section and began tuning her violin. The music was on the stands. At the director's request, all leaned forward, found the piece he asked for, and began looking it over.

Jean glanced toward the violins, where Bonnie Richardson sat very straight and attentive in the first chair. Bonnie was a tall, slim girl with soft brown hair and a sober, conscientious manner. She had sat in the third chair last year, with seniors occupying the first and second places. Now that they had graduated, Bonnie was the most likely candidate for the coveted position of concertmistress. Jean knew how much the position meant.

Mr. Friedman rapped for attention, raised his stick, and they began to play.

13

For Jean it was a thrilling experience to be playing for the first time with the orchestra. The harmonies swelled around her, and she concentrated on counting the measures to the point where she should bring in the drums. A trumpet lost the count, and she was aware of discords. Mr. Friedman stopped the piece and repeated the passage, with a smile of encouragement for the freshman who had gotten out of time.

To Jean he said: "You came in just right, Jean. Now, if you'll handle the drums like this —" he came over to the drums and demonstrated a few strokes, pianissimo and fortissimo — "the effect will be much better." She tried them the way he suggested, finding to her surprise that it was not as easy as it looked.

"Most of the time we shall have piano parts with the numbers," he said. "Then Jerry, over here, can take over the percussion." Jerry played a flute, but he had doubled at the percussion instruments whenever needed.

At the close of the hour Mr. Friedman looked at Kim.

"You play very well," he said. "Where did you study?"

When she told him, he raised his eyebrows in recognition.

"We are lucky to have you this year," he said. Jean smiled at Kim in congratulation, and then caught sight of Bonnie, who looked worried. Jean felt a pang of sympathy for Bonnie. The girl looked at Kim, and, glowing and self-assured, Kim smiled reassuringly. Unwillingly Bonnie smiled back, giving her the recognition due her. Then slowly Bonnie unstrung her bow and put her instrument away, keeping her head down and her face averted.

Jean and Kim walked back to the lockers together.

Kim walked very straight, looking as if she had gone to Sherwood High School all her life. Already she knew a dozen students to greet in the halls. Collecting her books to take home, Jean felt again that anticipation of excitement in the coming year, as if Kim's personality cast a strange light over the future.

Jeff met her at her locker, his arms full of books, ready to leave.

" Where were you at two o'clock? " he wanted to know.

" I was in orchestra," Jean said. " I forgot to tell you I changed my schedule. It's going to be wonderful, Jeff."

He was silent as she collected her books and started down the hall with him. Jean hardly noticed his silence, as she talked about the orchestra, about Kim, about the new teachers, about the wonderful weather.

It was still the end of summer, when all the trees were clouded faintly with gold and the leaves hung tired and aged, not yet ready to loose their hold. Daily a few more gave up and floated languidly to the ground. The sunlight that filtered through an almost invisible haze warned them to enjoy its warmth today; tomorrow it might be gone.

" I hope we have a day like this on Saturday," Jean remarked, as they stood on the corner waiting for the bus. Clusters of students walked up the street together, and overtones of their conversation drifted behind them. A couple of Nightingales passed Jean, with a waved greeting, on their way to meet the boys at the Ranch House. Last year Jean had spent too many afternoons there with them. She thought of how important the invitation to join the sorority had seemed last fall. Was it only a year ago? She had grown so much since then. Funny how you didn't know you were moving ahead until you looked back and discovered how far you had come. She watched the girls go on up the street with a fresh sense of freedom in not being tied to the sorority, and then she turned back to Jeff.

" What's happening Saturday? " he wanted to know.

" Jimmy's going to be eight this week," Jean said. " He wants a birthday party for all the boys in his third-grade room. Twelve little boys! Mother says she doesn't see how she can face it, but Jimmy has it all planned. Something's going to happen, but we haven't quite figured it out yet."

" Jimmy's a cute kid," Jeff said, grinning at his recollection of Jean's small brother. " I'll come along and steer the party. After all, I spent my summer surrounded with small boys. I ought to know how to get along with them. Why don't you and I take the gang out in the woods for a picnic? I could get the folks' station wagon."

" Oh, he'd love it! " Jean cried. " It would be wonderful if you would, Jeff. Mother would be so grateful to have it off her hands."

" How about you? " The question didn't seem like Jeff.

" I think even an eight-year-old boys' party could be fun if you were there," Jean told him.

" Do you mean that? "

Something in the intensity of his question struck her uncomfortably, and in her discomfort she chattered faster than ever, hoping she had been mistaken.

" What Jimmy wanted more than anything was a baseball mitt. He talked about it all summer. All the guys had one, he said, and he couldn't play ball with them without a mitt. But mitts cost about eight dollars, and Dad said he just didn't have that much to spend on a baseball mitt for a third-grader. Rick tried to cheer him up with his old one, but he'll need his own in the baseball season. We all felt kind of bad about it, and then last week Sally saw one reduced from eight dollars to three ninety-five, and we all chipped in and got it for him. He's going to be standing on his head when he sees it — especially since he's been told not to expect one."

Jeff laughed. " I can remember when I was about eight or nine," he said. " A baseball mitt is the most important thing in life, right then. I'm glad he's getting it. I'll bring him a ball to go with it. O.K.? "

He was sweet to suggest it, Jean thought, with a sudden rush of tenderness. Jeff was so nice about so many things.

" We'll have a date on Saturday night, as usual," he reminded her, as they parted at the corner. " But Saturday afternoon will be a bonus. With decent weather it ought to be good."

Jean walked down Juniper Lane in a glow of comfortable warmth. It was good to be Jeff's girl again. She had missed him so much last year. Now they were back in the old *status quo*. He was so dependable. And so unsentimental, she told herself, trying to believe it.

As she turned at her door to look once more at the yellowing trees, a handful of golden leaves brushed through the air, and inexplicably she was reminded of Kim Ballard. She had forgotten to ask Jeff what he thought of her. And that was funny, because Jean thought she was fascinating.

CHAPTER 2

THE Burnaby family celebrated Jimmy's birthday at supper Friday night with a decorated cake flaming with nine candles — eight for his age, and one to grow on. Ice cream had to be bought at the store this year, since Mr. Burnaby was unfortunately detained on the campus and there was no time for the traditional homemade ice cream in the hand-turned freezer that featured most birthdays.

"You lucky little boy," Jean observed, as Jimmy cut into his cake. "Two parties for one birthday, as far as I can see. How many kids are coming tomorrow?"

"Twelve," Jimmy said happily. "That'll make thirteen counting me." Jean shuddered. "Boy, are their eyes going to fall out when they see this mitt!"

He punched one fist into the palm of the new baseball mitt which he had carried to the table with him.

Sally smiled at him fondly. She was just enough older, Jean thought, to consider an eight-year-old boy amusing. Jean herself found him strenuous and frequently a nuisance.

"Is that the kind you wanted?" Sally asked. She had picked it out.

18

"This is better than the one I wanted," Jimmy said blissfully.

"I'll play ball with you after supper," Ricky offered.

Ricky was a swaggering freshman this year, feeling very important, although not quite big enough. He worried daily about his height, which was now five feet six, measured himself every other day, and kept asking his mother when he was going to "shoot up" the way he heard boys sometimes did. Now that his little brother was eight years old, tall for his age, and very sturdy, Rick took a kindly interest in coaching him in sports and a family pride in producing a champion.

"You've only got six years to go till you're in high school," he told his young brother. "You'll need all the practice you can get before then."

Professor Burnaby looked over his five children benignly. Slender and wiry himself, he still looked young, as Mother did, Jean frequently thought. His sandy hair was fading unobtrusively into gray, but you wouldn't notice it. His eyes were blue, and seemed to be smiling most of the time. He was a professor of English at Northern University.

"How old are you now, Rick?" he asked. "About fifteen?"

Rick's glance was pained. "I'm just going into high school."

"I thought you were fourteen last fall. Weren't you?"

"I'm going to be fourteen on November 21," Rick told his parent patiently.

"Well, I certainly thought you were fourteen last fall." Mr. Burnaby was bemused by this discovery, and the family all laughed. Dad's inability to keep the ages of his

19

children straight was a long-standing joke in the family.

"That would make Betsy eleven," he calculated, and they laughed again.

"Betsy was eleven on the Fourth of July," Sally counted for him. "She's going into sixth grade. Jean is seventeen and a senior in high school, and I'll be twenty in the spring and a sophomore at the university. We're all three years apart — remember?"

Professor Burnaby winked at his wife and ran one hand down the back of his sandy head.

"I thought I felt older this morning," he said. "When the youngest is eight, why, they're practically grown up — all of them. Don't you ever feel kind of wistful about tiny feet pattering around the house — grown and gone forever?"

"Not me," said Mrs. Burnaby promptly. "They aren't gone — they're just tramping instead of pattering. And, actually, they're more fun as people than they were as babies."

She smiled at her family, and Jean thought how young she looked, in spite of the grown family that her father described with such nostalgia. Slight and not very tall, she sat very straight, and her hair was as dark as ever, her smile as quick. Now she drew a deep breath of pleasure.

"Jean, I think it was simply wonderful of Jeff to take on this party. You can tell him from me that I think he's a very fine boy."

Jean laughed, pleased with her mother's approval.

"Just give us a good day tomorrow and it'll be a good party," she said. "Jeff likes little boys."

Saturday was all she could wish for, warm and sunny.

20

The sky was bluer, the clouds whiter, the trees more golden, than any other day she could remember. Jean spent the morning in the kitchen organizing the food for the party. Jimmy's orders were hot dogs to be cooked over an open fire, potato chips, ice cream, and cake. Without arguing with him, Jean added lemonade and carrot sticks.

In the back yard she could hear Jimmy shouting to Ricky: "Burn 'em in, Rick! Send me a fast one!" His demands were accompanied by the thud of the baseball as he caught it with the new mitt, and she looked out of the window marveling at how well he could catch and throw for his age. Yellow leaves covered the fading grass of the wide yard, and as she watched a handful fell slowly to the ground. There was a sweet tang of wood smoke in the misty air. She could hardly wait to get out to the woods. Gratitude and tenderness for Jeff's thoughtfulness filled her mind. In another hour he would be here.

At twelve sharp the yard was full of small boys, running, shouting directions, throwing and catching what looked like a dozen balls. Jean had forgotten that boys were so prompt when they came to a party.

The presents were opened, examined, and laid aside. The lunch was packed, and she was watching for Jeff to arrive when Jimmy strode in.

"What are we waiting for?" he wanted to know. "All the guys are here. Let's get going. We're hungry."

"Here's Jeff now," Jean said, jumping to her feet as a Ford station wagon stopped before the house. "Tell the boys to get ready to load."

Jimmy dashed to the back door shouting for his guests, as Jean went to the front door to meet Jeff and hand him the baskets of food.

"It's a howling mob," she told him. "My, I'm glad you're in charge!"

"Just leave everything to me," he said largely. "I know what boys want."

In the car he tossed a baseball to Jimmy.

"Birthday present, boy," he said. "To go with the new mitt."

"Gee, thanks," said Jimmy politely. "That makes three hard balls I got today."

Jean blushed for him, and Jeff winked at her. "You'll probably lose all of them," he prophesied comfortably. "Now quiet down back there," he began backing away from the curb. "Duck down so I can see out of the back window."

Six boys were piled two deep on the back seat, squirming and wiggling. Six more filled the middle seat, with one of them falling regularly off the edge of the seat onto the floor, protesting and arguing. Jimmy sat in front with Jean and Jeff and yelled back to his guests.

"I thought we were going to play football," a shock-headed boy announced from the back seat. "It's fall, isn't it?"

"We're playing baseball," said Jimmy. "It's my party, and I got a new mitt."

"And three new balls," Jeff said, *sotto voce*. "I've got some good games planned for the mob."

"We don't want any games," said Jimmy. "We're playing baseball."

They found a spot in the forest preserve where a baseball field was laid out near a fireplace and picnic tables, and the boys poured out of the car.

22

"Here," yelled Jeff, "help tote this food over to the tables."

But the boys had already scattered too far to hear him. In a huddle on the baseball field, they were arguing loudly over positions. Jeff turned to Jean with a baffled expression.

"I don't know what I'm doing here," he said. "They're going to run their own party anyway."

"You're here to help me carry the food," she said. "And build the fire, and see that they don't poke each other in the eye with their hot-dog sticks. You'll be plenty useful — behind the scenes."

They carried the wood they had brought for the fire, baskets of food, jugs of lemonade, picnic equipment, from the car to the picnic table a couple of hundred feet away. Jeff built a fire and Jean laid out the hot dogs, the roasting forks, buns, pickle relish, mustard, knives, cups, plates.

"Come and get it," Jeff bellowed.

Thirteen little boys dropped bats and balls and mitts where they stood and charged upon the picnic table.

"Now take it easy," Jeff sounded authoritative. "Hey, you, no shoving!" He dragged one little boy out from under the elbows of four others and set him in line. Another grabbed a hot dog and found that he was holding a string of four. He wrenched off one, and the others dropped to the ground. Jean groaned.

"Never mind," Jeff said, dusting them off. "They're going to be cooked anyway." He laid them back on the plate and tried to cut them apart before they would be snatched out of his hand.

Unexpectedly six little boys were roasting their hot dogs

fairly efficiently while six others stood around them, urging them to hurry up, clamoring about their hunger, advising them that their food was cooked, what were they waiting for? One stood by the picnic table eating potato chips as fast as he could stuff them into his mouth. By the time Jean noticed him, half the supply had disappeared.

Incredibly they were all fed without any casualties. The cake had been served, ice cream bars were passed out, and in a whirl of dust thirteen small boys left the shambles around the picnic table and reassembled on the baseball diamond, shouting directions to each other about beginning where they had left off.

Jean and Jeff sank limply on the benches and stared at each other.

"Look at this mess," she said, feeling exhausted. "Did the boys at camp act like this?"

"I should say not," Jeff said vigorously. "But at camp we had some discipline." He sounded as if something had been missing in the upbringing of this group.

"Well," Jean defended her family honor, "you can't expect discipline at a birthday party."

"I guess not," he said resignedly. "Well — let's eat ourselves. I'm starved, and we couldn't get a bite until those little cannibals were taken care of."

They searched through the remnants of food, and Jean laughed hysterically.

"They ate everything in sight," she said. "Luckily I kept back two hot dogs — "

"Only two?" Jeff sounded as aggrieved as a small boy himself. "I could eat at least four!"

"You can have mine," she offered. "I'm not very hungry any more."

24

" I should say not! "

They found a couple of buns, ate the crumbs of potato chips, and munched on a large number of carrot sticks which the boys had almost unanimously disregarded.

" You can fill up on cake," Jean comforted him. " There's plenty of that left. And then you'd better straighten out that ball game. They're wrangling again."

The game went on for two hours.

" What time had we better take them home? " Jeff asked Jean hopefully, at the end of that time.

Consulting her watch, she said, " It's 3:30. Let's wind up the game, and leave by four."

At quarter to four the game was concluded and the boys were advised to help load the car. It took five minutes to get them off the diamond, to give each a load to put in the car, and hand out the favors.

" All right, are we all here? " Jeff called. " Let's go, men! "

They raced pell-mell for the car, calling, " Dibs on the seat by the window," and found places with considerable argument, shoving, and finally compromise. Jean counted heads.

" Eleven," she said, after counting twice. " Who's missing? "

The boy in the far corner of the car, sitting under another boy, called out, " I think Tommy and Jay went to look at the river."

" Good heavens," Jean looked at Jeff, appalled. " You run and look for them and I'll stay with this mob."

" We'll find them! " All the boys began to climb out again.

" No you don't! " Jeff thrust them back in with a firm

hand. "Two missing is enough. You guys stay right here, while I get the others. Which way did they go?"

He strode through the woods in the direction of the river, while frantic fears raced through Jean's mind. She tried to think of last-minute things to check, telling herself there was no use worrying over the missing boys until Jeff returned. Turning to the boys who were momentarily quiet, she said, "Have we got all the bats?"

"I forgot mine. It's right over there on the diamond."

The boy next to the door was out before she could stop him, racing back to the playing field. She sighed and watched him, determined not to lose another one.

"My ball got lost, and I didn't have time to look for it," announced another boy.

"Well —" Jean tried to think of the best way to handle the situation, "all right. Two of you can look for the ball. But don't go away, any of you. Stay right in sight of the car."

Before she realized it, the car was empty again, and all the boys had reassembled on the baseball diamond. She walked over and joined them, trying to direct the search for the ball, and hoping that Jeff would get back soon with the missing two. Suddenly she felt very inadequate, in sole charge of eleven small boys.

"Here's the ball," announced one of them, running out of the woods. She hadn't realized he had gotten out of sight, and her relief at seeing him was mixed with consternation for fear another had gone.

"Everyone over here," she called. "Let's count heads again."

There were still eleven. And Jeff was still gone.

"Go ahead and play ball," she said. "But don't lose

the ball, and don't leave the game."

It seemed like an hour before she saw Jeff striding toward her with two small boys in tow. They had not only found the river, but they told her, with the nonchalant pride of successful adventurers, that they had fallen in, only it was almost dried up. She looked at them, caked with mud, and wondered what their mothers would say.

The car was loaded again, thirteen heads were counted, the doors were locked, and the car rolled out of the forest preserve. Suddenly all the boys were quiet, exhausted with the afternoon's activity. One by one Jeff found their homes and dropped them off. Unexpectedly each said, as he climbed out: "Thanks for the party. I had a swell time."

"Looking back," said Jean, when they stopped at the Burnaby house at quarter past five, "it was kind of fun, after all. But strenuous. You were just wonderful to do all this for my little brother."

"Believe me, I wouldn't have done it if he wasn't your little brother," Jeff told her with a tired grin. "I'll see you at 7:30 — if I can still walk."

"It'll be a quiet, peaceful evening," Jean promised him.

This was their first date since his return from vacation last Monday, although he had called her daily during the week. As she brushed her eyebrows, pleased that they were so well shaped, and fastened flowers in her hair before her mirror that night, Jean thought how pleasant her senior year was going to be, now that she could depend on Jeff again.

"I wonder if this is what love is like," she asked herself, and smiled at the question. "Enjoying being with someone so much, and yet no strings attached — just having fun together, and knowing what to count on."

When Jeff returned at 7:30, shining with soap and water and a fresh summer shirt, she thought again, with surprise, that she had never realized before how attractive he was. She liked to look at him, with that twinkle in his eye and the wry grin that always struck a chord of response in her.

They agreed about so many things: that little boys were exhausting, but cute, that the movie wasn't very good but next week's attraction sounded better, that Kim Ballard looked like an interesting person, that chemistry was a vitally important field of opportunity in the atomic world. Jeff planned to major in chemistry when he went to college. Neither Jean nor Jeff had decided yet what college each would choose.

They walked home from the movie in the warm September night and watched a lowering bank of clouds creeping up around the moon.

"It'll probably rain tomorrow," said Jeff, lounging comfortably on the old glider on the Burnaby screened porch. "We were just lucky to get a day like this afternoon for that affair in the woods."

Jean laid her head against the back cushion and squinted her eyes as she watched the moon through the screen. She sighed with contentment.

"I've got an idea," Jeff said, laying his hand on hers. "If you'll walk one block west and I walk two blocks east, we could meet on the corner to take the 7:30 bus for school together. Why not?"

"Why — " Jean was surprised for a moment, then flattered, and then amused. In all the time she'd known Jeff he had never been romantic, and here he was asking her to arrange to ride to school with him every morning. "I think that would be nice, Jeff. Let's put it this way. If I'm not on that corner, it'll be because I couldn't get started soon enough. Then I'll just grab the bus at the nearest corner and meet you on it. But most of the time I can walk down all right — I think."

"Swell," said Jeff contentedly. "I hope you realize what a sacrifice I'm making. I've been taking the eight o'clock bus all these years. And just for you I'll haul out of the feathers half an hour early. I think it would be kind of nice to see you in the mornings."

"Probably you think you'd better have a little more time at school for study," Jean teased him.

"No doubt," he agreed. "It's a deal, then."

"It's a deal," she told him, wondering why it meant so much to him to meet her in the mornings.

He turned toward her, suddenly serious.

"Jean," he said and her heart began to beat faster at his tone, "I wish we could go steady. Would you? I mean, I never wanted to before — but now I — well, after last spring I thought about this all summer, and then all this week since I've been home, and I want to go steady. I just feel that way about you —"

"Why, Jeff —"

He was looking at her very seriously, and Jean closed her eyes a minute, thinking hard. She had thought all this week that he was exactly the way he had always been, easygoing, lighthearted, humorous about serious things like study and love. And here he was not humorous at all.

She knew he was fond of her, and that she was very fond of him. But going steady was something else again. She had tried it last year, and she knew what the drawbacks were. But that was another boy.

With Jeff, why not? She knew that in spite of his easy-going fooling Jeff was surprisingly touchy and sensitive. Look how easily he had gotten mad at her last year over the sorority. She liked him and admired him, and there was no one else that she cared about. They were seniors now, and that made a difference. Didn't it?

"Why, Jeff, I didn't know you felt that way," she said softly.

"Well, it seems that I do," he said. "I just can't stand the idea of your going out with anyone else. There isn't anyone else, is there?"

"No," said Jean. "There never was, Jeff." She made up her mind quickly. "Yes, I'll go steady with you this year."

"Gee, that's wonderful," he said, as if he could hardly believe it. He leaned across and kissed her, and Jean wondered why she couldn't be more excited about this arrangement.

"Say," he leaned back against the glider again, "how come you aren't in the history class we planned to take together? I meant to ask you before, but we always seemed to get talking about Jimmy's party —"

"I told you I'd decided to take orchestra," she reminded him. "That meets at the time your English class comes. So I had to change English, and the only time I could get was ten in the morning, and that knocked out the history."

He looked unconvinced.

"Well — in our last year," he argued, "it's kind of too bad we couldn't do it the way we planned last summer —"

She might just as well give him all the bad news at once, she thought.

"I'm not going to take journalism either," she said. "I

thought we could work on the yearbook together, but that's out too."

"For Pete's sake, why?"

"I'm taking two music lessons a week this year," she told him. "And they have to come on Mondays and Thursdays. We tried to make it Wednesday and Saturday, but Miss Austin couldn't fit that into her schedule. And I'll be practicing two hours a day, now — so I'm just letting some of the activities go."

"Well, gee whiz," he expostulated, "this year isn't going to be any fun at all!"

She shrugged. "I found out during the summer that music is my future, and I'd rather practice now than write stories for the paper. You have to make those choices — there isn't time for everything."

"Oh, I think your music is swell," he assured her. "But does it have to take all the time there is?"

"I guess it does."

He was philosophical, but with a visible stoicism, and Jean had a foreboding of trouble, wondering, and trying not to notice her question, whether she would have to consider Jeff's reactions about everything she wanted to do. Ever since she had left the sorority she had enjoyed a sense of freedom and independence, and now for the first time since then she felt no longer like a free agent.

Perhaps it had been a mistake to agree to go steady with Jeff. But surely you didn't make mistakes so easily, by the time you were a senior.

CHAPTER 3

DESPITE Jeff's annoyance over her changed schedule, Jean looked forward to her music lesson on Monday afternoon with absorbing interest. Miss Austin's enthusiasm for Jean's progress during the summer was contagious, and at each lesson Jean was aware of a renewed surge of determination, and a deep satisfaction in having made up her mind about what she wanted to do with her life. She had practiced three hours on Sunday this week end, finally mastering an intricate passage in polyrhythm, and she could hardly wait to play it for her teacher.

At the close of the lesson Miss Austin said, a little hesitantly: "Jean, your work is just fine. I'm surprised every week at your progress this year. There is only one handicap, and perhaps it is not too important. But you should be practicing on a grand piano, if it is at all possible. Has your family ever considered getting one?"

Jean sat very still. She had not thought of a grand piano for herself because she knew the strain such an expense would be for her family.

"I don't see how we could get one, Miss Austin, with Sally in college and everything. We've never even talked about it — but, of course, I'd love it." As she spoke, a grand piano became terribly important, the one thing she had to have.

"Sometimes you can find one that somebody would like to store," said Miss Austin, "and then you have the use of it. A friend of mine — a music teacher — is going to sell her piano in a few months. She wants to go to Arizona and retire. It's a wonderful instrument — I'd love to see you have that one to work on."

"I'll talk to Mother and see what she says," said Jean, suddenly hopeful. "How much does she want for it?"

"It's Mrs. Turner's piano," said her teacher. "I don't know if she's set a price on it. I should think it was worth a thousand dollars."

A thousand dollars.

Jean walked home, her head spinning with conflicting thoughts. She knew how carefully they must budget, now that Sally was in college and she herself would be going next year. She knew there was not a dollar to spare. But sometimes miracles happened. She had about two hundred dollars that she had been saving since last year. Perhaps with more sitting and extra Christmas work she could earn another hundred before the piano was to be sold. A deep excitement welled up and broke into a wide smile at the thought. Nothing, but *nothing*, could be so wonderful as to have a grand piano.

Brownie, Ricky's little brown dachshund, came prancing down the street to meet her, and Jean knelt down and rubbed her ears.

"You cute thing," she said fondly. "Where's Rick?"

Brownie barked and danced around in a circle, as Rick rode up on his bicycle, loaded with evening papers.

"She's getting real dependable," he said proudly. "She'll

go right around the route with me now and not get lost at all. Come, Brownie! "

He hurled a rolled paper at the porch of the house in front of which they were standing and hit the front door with an accurate thump. Remounting his bike he rode on. Throwing papers without getting off his bike was a technique he had practiced for weeks. Brownie trotted behind him, head up, looking very businesslike until she saw a squirrel and chased it up a tree. By the time Ricky had gone three houses beyond her she left the squirrel and followed him.

" Cute dog," said Jean to herself, as she turned into her own walk. Brownie was one of the family now, and they all wondered how they had gotten along without her before.

"But, Mother! " Betsy was protesting as Jean opened the door, " I don't see how I can stand it much longer! I've got to start playing violin again. The orchestra will begin rehearsal in another week, and I'm in it."

Betsy's violin had been a source of amusement to Jean last spring. Her younger sister had practiced diligently on an instrument rented from the school, and Jean had considered that it sounded impossible, and was only a passing interest. During the summer Betsy had had no instrument, although she had inquired among the families of her friends to see if someone didn't have a violin she could borrow. By August she had resigned herself to wait until school opened, and Jean had almost forgotten about the violin.

" What's the trouble? " Jean asked, as she entered the living room and put her music on top of the old upright piano.

"They won't let me rent a violin this year," Betsy sounded bereaved. "They say you can only have one that way for one year, and then you have to get one of your own if you're going to keep on."

The implications of this statement struck Jean like a rush of cold water. She turned to her mother.

"But, Mother — I didn't think Betsy was really going to play that old fiddle — "

"I *told* you I was going to play," Betsy was on the verge of tears. "It was beginning to sound real good. Mr. Ryan said I should have lessons over the summer, but no one would let me."

"But, honey, I told you last year I didn't see how we could afford lessons for you and Jean both," said Mrs. Burnaby. "It's not too late — you can take the school lessons again, even if — "

"But I have to have my own violin," said Betsy. "I just have to get one — I don't see why I can't have a violin when they need me in the orchestra."

"If they need you so badly, I don't see why they don't supply the instrument," said her mother dryly. "Well, I'll talk to Daddy, and we'll see what can we can figure out. Here he is now."

"I can't wait much longer," said Betsy with an obstinate expression. "I waited all summer patiently, just because I thought I could catch up this fall — "

"Have we got another crisis?" asked Professor Burnaby, as his wife and younger daughter turned toward him.

Jean was thinking hard about her own problem. She had never dreamed that they would have to get another musical instrument. If a violin was out of the question, how could she ever expect to get a grand piano? She walked over to the old upright, and played some bass octaves. The action was loose and the bass notes sounded dead. She was positive that a violin could not mean as much to Betsy as the piano would to her.

"Just the budget again," said Mrs. Burnaby with a smile that looked forced. "Betsy thinks she can't live without a violin, and the school won't rent her one the second year."

"But when we let her get into the violin class last year we thought she could play a rented instrument through sixth grade and not get into the business so expensively. After all, with Jean taking two lessons a week and Sally's tuition this month — we're scraping bottom as it is."

"I know," said Mrs. Burnaby. "We couldn't afford another cent for a toy or a pastime. But if Betsy were really serious about this —"

"But, Mother, of course I'm serious!" Betsy cried passionately. "Haven't I been telling you all along how important it is?"

Mrs. Burnaby looked at her husband, who shrugged his shoulders. Jean stared at both her parents, and then at Betsy.

"In sixth grade everything is life-and-death serious," Mr. Burnaby remarked. "Remember that awful time when Sally thought her whole life was blighted because she didn't have the lead in the sixth grade play? She talked about it for the whole semester, but I never saw any indication that she was going to make the stage her life's work."

"I know," said Mrs. Burnaby again. "Problems, problems, problems. Listen, Betsy, Daddy and I will figure, something out. Now don't fuss at us — we'll tell you when we know what we can do." To her husband she said: "I think I'd better go and talk to Mr. Ryan. Maybe I can persuade him to let us have a violin just for this year, and then it will all blow over."

"You'd better go see him first thing tomorrow."

Betsy looked disappointed. "But I wanted one of my own," she mourned. "It's different when it's your own."

Jean tried to put the whole thing out of her mind. It was her parents' problem and Betsy's, and there was nothing she herself could do about it. But Betsy sounded as if it were so terribly important. Jean found herself wondering urgently about the violin as she hurried home the next day after school.

She was setting the table for supper when her father came home, and she could hear her mother telling him about the interview with the music supervisor. Stealing a glance at her parents, she thought her mother's expression was odd. Sort of incredulous and surprised, as if she didn't believe what she was saying, and yet could not entirely disbelieve it.

"Mr. Ryan says Betsy has a lot of talent," said Mrs. Burnaby the moment her husband came in the door. "I had a long talk with him this morning, and he says she should be having lessons — that she's got a great deal of promise, and we should develop it."

Mr. Burnaby hung his raincoat in the closet silently, returned to the living room, and sat down as if he were preparing himself to face something.

"Now, Sara," he said, as if he were trying to be very objective about the whole thing, "Mr. Ryan is just trying to cultivate some more strings for his orchestra. You mean we should get involved in another musical program, to the tune of hundreds of dollars, just because the orchestra director wants Betsy to play a violin? "

Mrs. Burnaby looked distressed. " That's what I thought, when he started talking," she admitted. " After all, there doesn't seem to be any reason why we should have a talent for violin in our family. Nobody is even musical except Jean — But the way he talked about it, I began to feel as if we were being stupid not to recognize a talent in one of our own children."

" Has he got any children of his own? " Mr. Burnaby demanded.

" Four," said his wife, " and every one of them plays an instrument. The youngest is seven, and she plays a violin beautifully. She happened to be there, and I heard her."

" Hm," said Mr. Burnaby. " Well — I don't know anything about talent. You do what you want to about it."

He began to open the evening paper, and then he laid it down again.

" How much is this all going to cost, anyway? " he asked. " Of course, if Betsy has really got something, she ought to have as much chance to develop it as Jean has had — "

" That's what I thought," agreed Mrs. Burnaby. " When Jean started lessons at nine, nobody ever said anything about talent, and she wasn't demanding to be taught at that time. And here's Betsy, nearly beside herself because she can't be playing a violin. Her music supervisor says she has this big talent — that's just what he said — ' the signs of a big talent.' " She repeated the supervisor's words in a tone that expressed at once pride and doubt. " It does seem as if perhaps we ought to try to give her the lessons she's asking for."

Mr. Burnaby raised the paper with a sigh.

"I don't care about a virtuoso in the family," he said, "and don't get any ideas about the concert stage. But if she wants to play a violin, go ahead, if you can get it out of the budget."

Jean, moving very quietly about the table, careful not to lose any of the discussion, was torn between excitement and alarm.

If Betsy had all this talent, she ought to be having lessons. She thought of Betsy's persistent work last year, her calm determination to be in the orchestra, her satisfaction over reaching her goal by the end of the year, and she could not escape the conviction that Betsy's music was at least as important as her own.

But what about that piano?

Betsy burst through the door, late from a scout meeting, and shouted, "Did you see Mr. Ryan?"

"Don't slam the door," said her father automatically, "and lower your voice. We're right here. You don't have to yell."

"Yes, I saw Mr. Ryan," said her mother.

"What did he say? Did he say I could play?"

"He says you should be having lessons," said her mother, carefully. "Daddy and I have been talking it over. We think perhaps you should. But I don't see how we can buy you a violin at this time. If you had to choose, would you rather have the violin or the lessons?"

"The lessons, naturally," said Betsy, immediately. "But what about the violin? Can I have one sometime?"

"I'll talk to Mr. Ryan again," said her mother. "Maybe he'll rent one for just one semester. He suggested that he might make an exception this one time, since there were a couple of instruments that were not yet assigned. He said if you could have the lessons he'd let you borrow the violin for a while."

" How soon can I start? "

" I'll ask him about a teacher," said her mother. " Now just relax and help Jean with the table."

Jean began to breathe more easily. Surely something would turn up so they could get both the violin and the piano. She had no idea how much a violin would cost — a little tiny instrument like that you ought to be able to get for less than a hundred dollars, she should think. She thought of the money she had saved, and wondered, for one wild, self-sacrificing moment, if she ought to offer to buy a violin for Betsy.

But if it were not necessary right now, if Betsy could rent a violin for a semester, maybe they could get the piano first and the fiddle later.

Then she put the violin out of her mind. She had to have that piano!

~~~~~~~~~

CHAPTER 4

~~~~~~~~~

THE school year moved into full swing with the half-forgotten momentum of other years. It was more important this year than ever before, Jean felt, that time should move slowly, that she should cling to every moment and savor every hour of high school life while she could. And yet time slipped away from her even as she clutched at it. She woke with a start one morning thinking: It can't be the fourth week of school already. It just can't be! There haven't been enough days for so many weeks. But by the time she arrived at school and met Kim Ballard at their appointed time at the lockers, it seemed, in odd contradiction, as if she had known Kim for years.

They ate lunch together every day, and the more Jean saw of Kim, the more compatible they found each other. Jean admired Kim's flashing personality and audacity, Kim admired Jean's quick wit and humorous comment on life in Sherwood High School. Jean just loved Kim's chestnut hair and Kim thought Jean had remarkable style, which, from a girl who had spent two years in France, Jean found very flattering. Kim made friends easily, and most of her classmates liked her, while Jean had always had many friends in the high school. Yet, as the days slid past, Jean found herself waiting for Kim at noon, meeting Kim after school, eager to exchange the day's news with Kim, and too busy with one thing or another to join her other friends very often.

She had told Kim all about her family, about her older sister in college, her younger sister who played the violin, her little brother who was a cub scout. Kim was fascinated with the large family that was outside her own experience, as Jean was fascinated with Kim's adventures in Paris and Berlin, with the man she thought she was in love with who sang in a Broadway show, with the famous persons she knew through her famous father. In spite of her glamorous life, Kim loved Sherwood; she thought Tony Latimer, one of Jeff's good friends, was wonderful; she thought Jeff was terribly nice. She was a most satisfactory person, Jean thought. She even thought Ricky Burnaby was cute, when Jean pointed him out in the hall one day.

"Cute?" Jean wondered, watching her brother swinging along with a cocky, confident stride and a breezy grin on his face. Well, maybe he was. She hadn't thought of it before, being more accustomed to seeing him unwashed, uncombed, and taken to task for being late to meals. Behind her and Kim a couple of freshman girls gasped and squealed.

"There's Ricky Burnaby!" one of the girls pretended to be stricken with excitement.

"Oh, no, where?" demanded the other. "My girl friend said she'd introduce me, and she never has!"

Jean was amused and a little surprised. Ricky took no interest in girls as far as his family were aware. The only concern in his life these days was making the freshman football squad. He had grown an inch this past month, and now stood at five feet seven and weighed in at one hundred and fifty pounds. He kept comparing himself with other freshmen. At last count there were six others on the squad no taller than he was. And there was always the chance that he would begin to "shoot up," although his mother pointed out that she didn't see how he could possibly grow any faster than he was now doing. Football was as important to him as his little brown dachshund, as Jimmy's baseball mitt was to Jimmy, as a violin was to Betsy; as important as Bob Carlson was to Sally.

Just how important Bob was to Sally, Jean was not prepared to say, although she had a feeling that he was The Man.

Sally was a sophomore at Northern University in Sherwood, where her father was on the faculty, majoring in English and taking a minor in education. Ever since she had been a senior in high school she had planned to teach, and now she talked about it as if she could hardly wait to begin. Slimmer than she had been in high school, as pretty as ever, with black hair that curled at the ends and a clear, fair skin, she was vivacious and impulsive still, but more mature. Jean thought frequently that Sally seemed entirely grown-up.

Last spring Jean had surmised that Sally would be wearing Bob's pin any week end, although Sally had told her a little scornfully that in college you didn't trade pins around as casually as you did in high school. Whatever it meant, Sally didn't have Bob's pin yet. But she talked about him as if they felt alike about everything; she made no plans, even with the girls, until she checked with Bob.

She put Bob ahead of everything else, Jean thought, as Jeff crossed the hall at an intersection, and waved to her. That was the way she was compelled to feel about Jeff — as if she ought to consider him ahead of everyone and everything else. The difference was that Sally wanted to think of Bob first, she just naturally thought of him first, and Jean only felt reluctantly as if she ought to.

It made her no happier to know that Jeff did not care much for Kim.

Once, in the first week of school, she had been afraid that he might like Kim too well. Now when she asked him why he didn't like her, he always protested that of course he liked her just fine. But Jean could feel a denial below his protestations. She herself found Kim more interesting as time went by.

Jean had been awed by Kim's exceptional accomplishment on the violin at first, and had worked harder than ever for a couple of weeks to match her on the piano. Now she found herself taking it for granted that Kim played astonishingly well, and she took great satisfaction in the fact that Kim liked her accompaniment and admired her piano-playing. They were a pair, and, Jean felt with pride, an accomplished and outstanding pair.

In the third week of October all members of the orchestra tried out for the positions they would hold for the rest of the year.

Kim took the first chair in the violin section easily. No one was surprised, but Bonnie Richardson was so disappointed that she could hardly keep back the tears. Jean liked Bonnie, and ached for her disappointment. But what could you do with competition like Kim? Even Bonnie acknowledged bravely that no one could play like Kim.

She took the second chair and co-operated in a steady, dependable fashion. And when Kim missed two after-school rehearsals in the same week Bonnie led the violins in her place.

The orchestra director seemed annoyed at Kim's absence, although she gave him a written excuse each time. Jean thought Mr. Friedman was unreasonable. Kim didn't need the practice, and with Bonnie taking her place the orchestra didn't suffer. Why did he have to be like that about his most talented violinist?

Kim told Jean, laughing at the humor of it, that she had never worked the way her teacher had wanted her to.

"M. Renard, in Paris, was always saying, 'But, Mademoiselle, you have the big talent, *le talent magnifique!*'" She rolled her eyes and threw out expressive hands. "When he found I was playing a better lesson than usual, and had only practiced two hours in the whole week, he'd wring his hands and hold his head. He wanted to drive me — and no one can drive me! If talent is supposed to drive me, I think it's just a kind of nuisance."

Something in Jean rejected Kim's airy nonchalance about talent, but she hardly recognized the dissenting whisper. No matter how casual Kim was about it, Jean admired her talents deeply.

Kim went on: "What I really want to do is to go on the stage — and someday maybe I will — who knows? Nick said he could do something for me there."

Nick was her love in the chorus of the New York play, and Jean was already accustomed to the idea of being the good friend of a girl who had a friend on Broadway. Someday, she thought, Kim will be on Broadway.

With all this glowing promise before her, Kim was like

any other high school girl, only more interesting. She seemed to like Tony, here in Sherwood High School, as well as she liked Nick on the New York stage; she had as much fun when she went out with him and Jean and Jeff on their frequent double dates and she giggled and teased like any other high school girl. Jean thought their dates had never been so hilariously entertaining, so full of fun and zany gags and jokes, as they had been since Kim and Tony joined them.

Why, then, was Jeff's dislike becoming more noticeable, at least to Jean?

"She wears me out," Jeff grumbled, when Jean said once that she thought he had seemed very quiet, and asked what was wrong.

"But didn't you think her impersonation of Miss Tappan directing a play was wonderful?"

"Oh, she's good, all right. But you can't ever get away from it. I mean, you have to keep noticing and laughing, and no one else gets a chance to say anything. I mean, once in a while I like a kind of quiet conversation."

"But everybody keeps on talking," Jean protested. "She doesn't monopolize."

"Oh, she doesn't intend to monopolize," Jeff conceded. "It's just that she's got that kind of personality. It wears me out, that's all!"

Jean did not realize what Jeff could not put into words: that when the four were together Jean paid more attention to Kim's antics and entertaining company than she did to him. Jeff wanted Jean to have eyes for no one else, to feel about him as he did about her, and when the four went out together Jean had too good a time laughing at Kim to devote very much time to her date.

46

When he waited for her to walk down the hall to their first class, Jean and Kim always came out of the home room together, usually completing plans for walking to the shopping district after school or getting together to practice the new piece they were playing together. When school had started Jean had walked to the bus with Jeff almost every afternoon, or they had gone to the Ranch House regularly on Wednesdays. But in the past weeks Kim had been included in their walks after school, and on the last two Wednesdays Jean had had to stay for orchestra rehearsal for the fall concert, and had run laughing up the stairs to the music department with Kim, while Jeff went out to take the bus alone. She had no idea that he felt neglected, and considered Kim a nuisance and an interruption.

When he asked her to go to the Homecoming Informal, the first big dance of the season on October 25, she said, " Maybe Kim can stay with me that night, and you boys can pick us both up at my house."

Jeff was silent a minute. Then he said: " Do we have to go with them everywhere we go? I thought this time we might just go by ourselves."

" Why, I thought you liked Tony," said Jean. " We've had so much fun with them. Don't you think double dates are more fun than going alone? "

" No, I don't," Jeff said flatly. " They're all right once in a while. But sometimes I like a change."

" But if we're all going to be at the same dance," Jean pointed out, " I don't very well see how we could just say we'll see them there — after all the fun we've had together."

" Do we have to be stuck in a habit? " Jeff sounded

angry. " I'll just tell Tony we're going alone this time and he can tell Kim. Anything wrong with that? "

" If that's the way you want to arrange it, there's nothing *wrong*," said Jean icily. " But I just can't see why you don't like Kim."

" O.K. O.K." he surrendered. " You fix it up any way you want it and let me know what's going on."

Really, boys could be so tiresome, Jean thought, calling Kim that night to invite her to spend the night of the Homecoming Informal with her. If Jeff kept on complaining like this, it could spoil everything.

As it turned out, there had been no need to argue at all. Kim was going out of town with her parents for the week end, and would not be going to the dance. When Jean reported this development to Jeff, she was pleased that he said only: " O.K., then. I'll pick you up at 8:30." If he had betrayed too much satisfaction, she would have quarreled with him again, she thought.

It was kind of nice after all, to date Jeff alone, she realized, the night of the dance. They talked about things they had not discussed for weeks. He was very much interested in the orchestra concert coming up the following week on Sunday afternoon, and Jean promised this year to turn in a big list of magazine subscriptions in the annual drive two weeks later, to make up for her defection of last year. They talked about college and musical and science scholarships, and stood in groups and chatted with couples they had not seen outside of school for a long time. Jeff's dancing seemed smoother and more inventive than ever, and he was lighthearted and gay.

It was a most satisfactory evening, in a quiet way, and as they drove home in Jeff's station wagon, Jean thought, although she would have not said so, that she knew what he meant about their dates being more wearing when the other couple were with them.

When he kissed her good night, he stood looking down at her for a moment.

"This has been a wonderful evening, Jean," he said. "Let's do it again this way some time."

He really was sweet, she thought fondly, and perhaps she hadn't been as nice to him as she should have been.

"I just loved it, Jeff," she said softly. "It was perfect."

He held her tight and kissed her again, and, still holding her, he looked into her eyes for a long moment. He cared more than she did, Jean thought uneasily. She liked him well enough to enjoy being with him, well enough not to want to hurt him. How much more did his feeling demand?

She turned and waved from the door as he went down the steps, bouncing lightly as if he felt good about something, and then she closed the door behind her and leaned against it for a minute, thinking. If Jeff cared too much about her and disliked her best friend, what was going to happen? And what could she do about it?

~~~~~~~~~

CHAPTER 5

~~~~~~~~~

JEFF was head of the magazine campaign for the school this year, and Jean spent the last week of October calling on all her parents' friends for magazine subscriptions. Mindful of last year's failure to produce because of sorority demands on her time, she devoted almost every waking moment to the effort and studied in the evening hours when it was too late to call on neighbors. She dragooned Kim into the campaign also, and persuaded her to work so effectively that Kim turned in $365 worth of subscriptions, topping Jean's figure of $325.

When Jean congratulated Kim, hoping privately that this production record would change Jeff's mind about her, Kim said lightly: " Oh, it wasn't any trouble! I just talked to Dad and he got subscriptions from everyone on the paper." Jean suppressed the unworthy thought that everything seemed to come to Kim easily. She herself had let her practicing go all week, and now that she had paid off the debt she felt she owed to Jeff from her junior year, she was going to let nothing more interfere with her music. It was more important than school offices or activities, and she was going to put it first.

Barbara Keller, tall and fair and popular, stopped by her

table in the cafeteria the day the magazine campaign closed. Barbara and Jean had been good friends last year, especially after Jean had broken with the sorority group.

"Aren't you going to be on the yearbook staff this year?" Barbara asked, smiling down at her. Barbara was editor of the yearbook. "I've been looking for you, Jean. I thought we'd have fun working together."

Jean looked up at Barbara, wishing she could be two people at once.

"I was planning to," she said. "But this year I'm practicing so much that I'm cutting out almost all activities. Orchestra and music are taking more time than I expected."

Barbara nodded understandingly. That was the nicest thing about Barbara. She could always understand another point of view.

"Well, nobody can do everything – and music is awfully important. Have fun, and we'll get together someday."

Watching her move down the cafeteria aisle, talking to someone at almost every table she passed, Jean felt a spasm of regret that she would not be working with Barbara this year. She liked her so much. She wondered if Kim were taking time that she could be giving to the yearbook. But the time she spent with Kim, Jean decided, would not have fitted a school activity anyway. There were actually only those afternoon walks to town when she was on her way home to practice, and a shopping trip about once a week, which she would have had to make for her own needs. And Saturday mornings, when she went in to Chicago with Kim occasionally.

Kim was stimulating company, with her wide range of

reminiscences and ingenious ideas for diversion. Last week she had suggested that they spend Saturday going through the Art Institute. While Jean had gone to the Art Institute twice in her life on conducted tours, it had never before occurred to her to go there on her own just because it was fun.

Kim compared the Art Institute with the Louvre in Paris, and told Jean of the thrill in seeing the Winged Victory for the first time. She was interested in the Spanish painters represented in Chicago, Velázquez, and Picasso, Goya and El Greco, pointing out colors and techniques Jean had never known before. She was excited about the sculptures of Meštrović, and revealed that her mother was a sculptress too, and one of her works was in the Art Institute.

" This is a wonderful town," she said, as they walked back to the subway. " It keeps surprising you in a different way from any other town I've lived in. Parts of it are so ugly, and other parts are so beautiful, like your Outer Drive along the lake."

It was an exhilarating day, and Jean felt as if she were touching new horizons of interest and knowledge that before she had only dimly imagined. She had always wanted to travel and to see great art museums and historic monuments, and here was Kim showing her almost in her own home town things that to a traveled person were as exciting as anything else she had seen.

Another Saturday Kim invited Jean to accompany her on a modeling assignment. She was driving down that day in her father's car, and Jean was enthralled with the anticipation of a strange, glamorous world of lights and make-up.

The famous photographer Gabriel met Jean politely and then said to Kim: " Did you know you're twenty minutes late? We'll do the pose in evening dress first, so hurry up and change."

Kim said apologetically, " I couldn't park this morning — "

" Nobody but a chump would drive down to the Loop on Saturday," he said in some annoyance. " O.K., try to change in five minutes, and let's not lose any more time."

Kim looked beautiful in evening dress, Jean thought, sitting in a corner on a stool and watching the photographer adjust lights. Kim had to stand, first with her hands arranged so the light would catch skin texture, then in a dancing position with a man dressed in a dinner jacket. It took forty-five minutes before ten pictures were taken, and Jean could feel the heat of the lights even where she sat in a dark corner.

At the end of forty-five minutes, the photographer said: "Did you bring the sports outfit? I got a rush order for a sunburn ad — "

" I brought it," Kim said. She disappeared again to change, while the men sat around discussing poses and lights and the vagaries of advertising make-up men. Then Kim reappeared with an eyeshade, swinging a tennis racket.

" We'll have to take off the eyeshade," said Gabriel. " Shadow's all wrong. Now make like you're sunburned and this cream is just what you're looking for."

It took a dramatic flair, Jean thought, as well as being photogenic. It also took six different poses with the tennis racket, timed and held for several minutes each, before Gabriel was satisfied. Kim looked tired, when at last she

53

joined Jean in her street clothes, ready to leave.

"O.K.," said Gabriel, turning off the bright light. "I'll let you know when I've got another assignment for you. And next time try to be on time, will you?"

It would have been pleasant, Jean thought, if he had stared at her and said: "Where have you been all the time? I've got just the thing for you —" She dreamed for a moment of being photographed at the keyboard of a grand piano with the top raised, and perhaps an enthralled group of listeners in the foreground. Kim had told her once that they paid her twenty dollars an hour for this job, and Jean thought now how much the money would mean to the Burnabys in terms of music. A piano and a good violin both.

But Gabriel showed no interest in her at all. He said only: "Nice to meet you, Miss Burnaby. Come with Kim any time."

At least he was cordial, Jean thought; at least he didn't tell her not to come. And she realized after watching this session that modeling was not so much glamour and fun as good hard work. But it did take some kind of talent, and she was awed by Kim's ability to do so many different things. She loved these Saturdays in Chicago.

The next week Kim had to go down earlier than Jean could leave Sherwood, and she invited Jean to meet her at Marshall Field's for lunch at one o'clock and shop for a new suit with her afterward.

Mrs. Burnaby demurred at the idea of Jean's spending every Saturday in Chicago on some pretext or other.

"There are lots of things you could use Saturday for right at home," she said. "I don't see why this has to be a weekly affair."

"It isn't *every* week," Jean said. "It just happens this one time to be three weeks in a row. And I'd be going to the football game if it were here in Sherwood. We can't go next week because that's the last game of the season, and Kim has looked all over Sherwood and couldn't find a suit. Besides there's a sale on, and maybe I could find something myself."

Her mother gave up the argument. "This one time," she conceded. "And then I should think you could save these city excursions for the holidays. When do you expect to be home?"

"I'll be back by five," Jean said.

Her mother just didn't understand, Jean thought, as she hurried for the interurban. This was the first year she had been going to Chicago so often, and the city still held for her all the excitement of a strange new town, with areas of exploration inviting her back again and again. Every time she went in to Chicago, she loved all the bustle and confusion and exhilaration of crowds of people going about their business, strings of traffic inching slowly toward their destinations, a beautiful sky line behind a beautiful water-front park, a city that was growing and changing and alive. And back of the busyness and the crowds were the concerts and the art exhibits and young people making ready to climb to the top and demand the attention of these crowds.

Jean made her way through congested aisles at Marshall Field's to a crowded escalator, and slid slowly up to the third floor, looking back at the milling people below her. On the third floor she found the waiting room and settled down with a magazine. She was five minutes early.

At 1:15 she sat up and looked around. It was not possible that Kim could have missed her. They had met here before and both knew the meeting place well. A little uneasy, Jean laid down her magazine and watched the big clock. Kim was frequently late. It was a failing Jean had tried to ignore, reasoning that no one could be perfect, and Kim had so many other good qualities that she could afford one shortcoming.

At 1:30 she rose and paced around the waiting room, wondering where she could look for Kim. Suddenly the city seemed less familiar and less friendly. Suppose they missed each other entirely and Jean had to ride back to Sherwood and explain to her mother that she had wasted three hours for nothing. She wondered how long she should wait. Her mother would have left before this, Jean knew. Mrs. Burnaby had no patience with tardiness prolonged beyond five minutes.

At 1:45 she gathered up her gloves and bag and stood irresolute. She must have misunderstood Kim about the meeting. She might as well go on and look for a suit alone, and try to justify her being down here today. But she was reluctant to leave alone.

At that moment a strange, impersonal voice spoke loudly and clearly through the waiting room. "Paging Miss Jean Burnaby. Please come to the information desk."

Her cheeks hot with the embarrassment of being thus publicly identified, Jean made her way quickly to the information desk.

"I'm Jean Burnaby," she said. "Were you paging me?"

"Telephone message," the clerk at the desk said impersonally. "Miss Ballard will be here in fifteen minutes."

"Thank you." Jean looked at the clock. Then she sat down and tried to compose herself.

At two Kim had not yet arrived. But this time she was definitely coming, Jean reminded herself. All she had to do was wait. Jean could not help thinking of all the things she might have done, had she stayed home this afternoon. There was mending accumulated from three weeks back, and she needed socks before Monday. There was extra practicing on a piece that she was anxious to work up. But she told herself in justification there was that suit she could use, if she could find a bargain. That was her reason for being here.

Kim arrived at ten minutes after two, and for the first time in their acquaintance Jean was a little annoyed with her friend.

"I'm terribly sorry about this," Kim said in abject apology. "I was just passing a window with the most marvelous buy in a taffeta dress, and I went in to ask about it and got stuck with the slowest, stupidest clerk! I got the dress on, and then I couldn't find the clerk, and when she showed up she had three other dresses to show me. I thought I'd never get away."

"Did you get it?" Jean asked, noticing the absence of packages.

Kim shook her head. "After all that, it wasn't quite right, and they offered to alter it, but things are never the same after changing, so I just let it go."

But did all of that business take an hour? Jean wondered. For the first time she began to see a flaw in Kim, and loyally she tried to shut her mind to it.

But it was not so easy to forget. Kim insisted on lunching at Field's, as planned, where by 2:15, service was slow. Kim didn't mind, claiming that her busy morning had fatigued her and she needed both food and rest. When they left the lunchroom it was after three, and Kim still had to hunt through the suit department. Without looking at suits Jean felt that she would have no reason to be with Kim today at all. So they went to the sixth floor and looked through not only one suit department but four. After Jean had tried on and rejected one suit, and Kim had rejected six, Jean insisted on starting for home. She knew by that time that she was going to be late and her mother's annoyance would reflect on Kim.

As Kim looked as the seventh suit and began to take it from its hanger, Jean said: "I'll have to go on, Kim. Mother expects me back by five, and it's already four."

"Well, I might as well go with you," Kim said. "I've seen everything. I wonder if I ought to take this gray flannel on trial —"

"It's a beautiful suit," Jean said, "but don't you think it is kind of expensive?"

Kim shrugged. "Oh, it's expensive, but I've looked at everything else, and I guess that's what I'll have to pay to get anything I like. Well — if I don't take this one I'll have nothing to show for all this time, and I can't come down next week. Wait just one minute and I'll dig up our clerk and tell her to send it out."

Jean waited, wishing Kim had made up her mind half an hour ago, since the gray suit was the first one she had tried on. In an access of consideration, Kim insisted on finding the clerk who had first shown it to her, and who was now busy with two other customers. And then, remembering that she was going to a reception with her parents the next afternoon, she said she thought she'd take it with her, which meant waiting for it to be wrapped. By the time they left the store it was four thirty.

When Jean got home it was quarter of six.

"But you said you'd be here by five," said Mrs. Burnaby in some annoyance. "What happened this time?"

"Oh, it was just one of those things," Jean said, trying to be indefinite about details. "Kim got involved with a dull clerk, and it made her late for lunch. You know how it is, Mother. You just can't do a thing if a clerk is keeping you waiting. And then when we found the suit she wanted it took hours to find a clerk to wrap it for her —"

"All I know," said her mother, "is that every time you are out with Kim either she keeps you waiting or you are late getting home. It's never been this late before, but it's always ten or fifteen minutes. I think the girl is irresponsible."

"O Mother, ten minutes is not important," Jean defended Kim. "And this is the only time she's ever been as late as this!"

"Ten minutes may not be an important amount of time," her mother agreed, "but it's the principle of the thing: the idea that no matter when she says she'll be somewhere, it really doesn't matter if she comes at another time. I call it irresponsible and I don't like it."

The flaw in Kim was not as bad as her mother described, Jean insisted to herself. She always kept her appointments, even if she was — well, call it casual about the exact moment.

When she talked to Kim about getting together on Friday evening, Jean had at the back of her mind, trying not notice it, a compulsion to prove that Kim was not irresponsible, to make Kim aware how important it was for Friday evening to move on schedule, and yet not let Kim think Jean was making too much out of it. The Y club was meeting at Jean's house for a potluck supper meeting, and Kim was cohostess with Jean.

"Then you'll be here at five," Jean said on Wednesday night, after a long discussion of details, "and bring along the dessert. I can take care of the other things. But if you can come right at five, we can set up the serving table and the card tables before the girls come at six."

"Right on the dot," Kim promised. "And I'll bring the ice cream." Jean had suggested that Kim bring an item that she could pick up easily at the store, knowing that Kim's hotel apartment made it difficult for her to prepare the gelatin salads or hot casseroles that other members of the club brought. The potluck suppers, which occurred about three times during the year, were undertaken by six members at a time.

When the telephone rang at five o'clock Friday afternoon and Jean heard Kim's voice, she was somehow not surprised.

"Say, Jean, would it make too much difference if I didn't get there tonight after all? Something has just come up and I can't get out of it. I'm terribly sorry. But I talked to Helene, and she's going to bring the ice cream and help with the tables. See you later — "

Jean hung up the telephone feeling frozen, and wishing her mother didn't have to know about this. The younger children were eating their supper in the kitchen to leave the dining room ready for Jean's supper party, and she went quietly to the sideboard and took out the lace cloth for the table. Some moments later her mother came to the door.

"Are you setting the table already? I thought Kim was going to help you."

60

" She can't get here after all. Something came up."

Jean moved busily from cupboard to table, setting out mats for the hot dishes, serving spoons for the salads, wondering how long it would take to set the card tables alone, how soon Helene would come.

" Really," Mrs. Burnaby sounded exasperated, " I wonder if you can count on Kim for anything at all! "

" O Mother! " Jean tried to keep her irritation out of her voice, " I wish you wouldn't always be picking on Kim. With the kind of family she has, things always do come up — it's the kind of life she leads. She called Helene to bring the ice cream in her place, and come early to help with the tables. And as far as setting the tables is concerned, it's nothing at all. Lots of the girls have to skip Y meetings more often than Kim does."

Her mother said no more and went back into the kitchen to give the children their dessert. Jean felt out of sorts and depressed with the effort attendant on being a hostess. She still believed in Kim, and she wished her mother would not keep pointing out every little thing that proved her own argument.

But down underneath, try as she would to ignore it, Jean could not help beginning to wonder if her mother were not right.

CHAPTER 6

BY early November Betsy's progress on the violin was apparent to everyone, although her family still found it difficult to believe that a Burnaby was actually "talented." Jean heard her mother, more than once, telling one of her friends, or Mrs. Scott next door: "We're amazed too. But her teacher says that Betsy can do anything she chooses someday — she's really got a great deal of talent. Of course we aren't thinking much farther than next year yet. If she will work hard and keep up this interest I suppose time will tell. But her teacher is astonished at the progress she's made."

Jean squirmed when she heard her mother, with that unhappy feeling that parents should never tell their neighbors how outstanding their own children are, and yet recognizing her mother's effort in convincing her friends to convince herself. She could not remember if her mother had ever talked about her that way: certainly never in her hearing. Her piano-playing had been taken for granted for a long time, and no one was surprised that she played well enough to be soloist for the high school orchestra. If there was a submerged pique in her recognition of a rival for musical honors right in her own family, Jean was trying hard to overcome it, and never admitted even to herself that Betsy's talent might interfere with her own needs.

She sat down at the old piano one day and found that one of the keys was dead. The old thing was getting worse every day, and she didn't see how she could stand it much longer. She leaned her elbows on the keyboard and put her head in her hands, thinking with painful intensity about the grand piano that her teacher wanted her to have.

Her mother was coming in the door, her arms full of bundles, and Jean raised her head. A cold wind swept in as the door opened.

"Mother, this piano is getting impossible. Did Miss Austin talk to you about that piano a friend of hers is going to sell?"

Even as she spoke, she felt guilty about asking her parents to spend more money, knowing how tight the budget was. But her need for a piano at that moment was overwhelming. The cold November air settled about her ankles, and she shivered a little.

Her mother dropped the packages on the table in the hall and closed the door.

"She called last month," Mrs. Burnaby said. "I told her I didn't see how we could possibly buy a grand piano at this time. After all, Jean, just try to be reasonable about this. Betsy's lessons are another hundred and fifty dollars a year we hadn't counted on."

"Yes, I know." Jean let her voice fall in despair. "But this piano is getting so bad. Look — this key is dead now, and it seems as if it's in every other chord I play. And the pedal squeaks —"

She pumped the pedal up and down, and certainly it did squeak badly.

"I'll get the tuner in as soon as I can," said Mrs. Burnaby. "It just seems as if everything happens at once, I don't know why. But I'm sure he can fix the key and pedal. This was a good piano once, and if we could just get through this year —"

"Then I'll be going to college," said Jean, "and we'll have two college tuitions instead of one! Maybe Betsy can earn some money professionally in about five years, and get the piano for me!"

Her mother looked as if she was going to reply sharply to Jean's bitter comment, when the telephone rang and she turned to answer it.

"Oh, yes, Miss Kimball! Yes, we do feel very much pleased with Betsy's progress . . . Well, I don't quite know how that can be managed. I can see what you mean, but still — Well, we'll have to talk it over and try to figure something out, but I really think — Oh, in that case, yes, thank you for calling. Good-by."

She turned back to Jean with a stricken expression.

"Betsy's teacher says Betsy will simply have to have a better violin than that school instrument. She says the child really ought to have one of her own, anyway."

Jean cleared her throat, feeling strangled.

"How much is that going to cost?"

"She said we might get a violin for $100 if we were lucky. The bow will be around thirty, and the case at least twenty-five." She hung up her coat, put away her purse and gloves in the drawer of the hall table, and faced Jean, daring her to be adult about this problem. "What did I say about everything happening at once? And Betsy needs a new winter coat this year — she's grown so fast."

"Mother, there is a perfectly good coat of mine hanging in the moth closet," Jean felt outraged. "It's just her size. Betsy doesn't like it, but it's a good coat anyway."

"I'd forgotten it," her mother looked relieved. "Well, that helps anyway. Honey, I'd love to have a grand piano myself. But I just don't see where the money will come from this year."

Jean sat still for a long minute, thinking about things. She didn't see where the money was coming from either. Well, she had the final choice of refusing to study music any longer or working with the piano she had. She raised her hands and struck the loud minor chords of a malagueña. Brownie, dozing on the rug beside the piano, sat up and rubbed her ear. Jean laughed at the little dog. "What's the matter, Brownie? Don't you like music?"

But it was not the music that bothered Brownie. She kept rubbing her ear all evening, and when Rick touched it unintentionally, she yelped.

"Say," he looked at the dog with sudden alarm. "I bet Brownie's got something wrong with her ear. Notice how she squawked when I touched it? And she keeps rubbing it."

Mrs. Burnaby knelt down to look at the dog, which drew away and whimpered at her touch.

"I'll take her out to the Animal Hospital first thing in the morning, Rick," she said, getting up again. "They can fix her up right away. Don't worry."

"Sure you won't forget?" he asked. "After all I've heard of dogs dying from ear infections. You think she can wait till tomorrow?"

His mother looked at the dog thoughtfully.

"She'll be all right for tonight," she said at last. "The hospital isn't open at this time of the night. Now try not to worry, Rick, and get your Latin done."

"Latin!" he groaned. "I don't see how I can concentrate when Brownie is dying at my feet."

"She's not dying," said his mother firmly. "And unless you get that Latin done, and done well, you'll be feeling worse than Brownie, because you'll be off that football squad faster than you ever got on."

Even the football squad could not prevent Rick from racing home the next afternoon to get the report on Brownie. He and Jean arrived together, and Jean found herself almost as alarmed as Ricky, although she kept telling herself that there was nothing at all to worry about.

"How's Brownie?" Rick shouted, as he slammed the door open until it hit the wall.

"She's going to be all right," his mother said from the kitchen. Rick sighed in loud relief and went out to the kitchen to revive himself with milk and fruit. Jean, following him, saw him look calculatingly at the cookies which he would have eaten by the dozen last year, struggle with the temptation to break training because it was so late in the season, and finally settle down with three bananas.

"Where is she?" Jean asked.

Mrs. Burnaby had her lips set as if she were braced to withstand any number of blows.

"Her ear was very bad," she reported. Rick's head jerked up in fresh alarm. "She has to stay out there at least a week. They're giving her sulfa injections, and the doctor says she'll be just fine without any question. But she'll have to stay until it's cleared up."

Rick accepted this philosophically, muttering only, "Poor little pooch, I'll bet she's lonesome."

But Jean delved straight to the point that worried her because she knew it worried her mother. "How much is *this* going to cost?"

"Thirty-five dollars."

"Thirty-five dollars!" Jean echoed. But Brownie was one of the family. "Well — I don't suppose there's anything else we can do —"

Rick gulped half a glass of milk. "We gotta take care of her," he said. "Say, Mom — I've got ten dollars left, after I got that new jacket last month. Suppose they'd let me pay it off on the installment plan?"

His mother smiled at his offer, but she shook her head. "Not if they operate like most hospitals," she said. "We'll talk it over with the family and see how we can arrange things."

"How's Brownie?" Betsy wanted to know, coming in late from school.

"How's Brownie?" demanded Jimmy, arriving from his den meeting.

"How's Brownie?" asked Sally, her arms filled with books from library study an hour later.

"What's the report on the dog?" Mr. Burnaby wanted to know as he sat down at the table.

"We've got to discuss more problems than Brownie," Mrs. Burnaby said after Brownie's condition had been reported four times. "It's all well and good to say that Brownie must be taken care of. I'm delighted that you are all so fond of the dog. But it's going to cost thirty-five dollars and I haven't got that much extra in the budget this month. Betsy's teacher says she's got to have a violin.

And Christmas is coming. Something's got to give."

There was a silence around the table. Sally was looking pensively out of the window where the world looked bleak and chilly in mid-November. Jean stared at the flowered wallpaper, following the pattern as it repeated itself over and over in medallions of roses. Betsy ate thoughtfully.

Sally spoke first. "I've got some money, Mother. I can let you have twenty-five dollars on that hospital bill."

"Thank you for offering, Sally," Mrs. Burnaby spoke gently: "But weren't you getting a new formal for the Christmas dance?"

Sally shrugged. "I thought a new one would be nice, but after all I've got two others, and they're both becoming. And Bob won't care whether it's new or old. He likes the blue one, anyway."

"That would take care of Brownie," Mrs. Burnaby said. "I hate to take your money, Sally, but there isn't much choice."

"That's O.K.," said Sally. "This is a family project, it seems to me. Bob said once that the nicest thing about my family is the way we all help each other out in a pinch."

"I've got ten," Rick reminded his mother. To Sally he said: "I can pay you back out of my paper money, Sal, but it may take a long time. Anyway, thanks."

Betsy raised her eyes from her plate where she had been thoughtfully pursuing peas with her fork.

"You know that awful old coat of Jean's that I hate?" she asked blandly. "If I can have my own violin, I'll wear that instead of getting a new one."

"Well, thank you for that fine offer," said Mrs. Burnaby, trying to accept Betsy's dictum in the spirit in which it was made. "I never could see what was wrong with that coat. It's a very nice tweed coat, I always thought."

" It scratches," said Betsy. " I tried it on once. And it makes me look fat. Besides, it's an icky tan color, and I wanted dark green, like all the girls are wearing this year. But," she concluded magnanimously, " I'll wear it anyway. It would be worth anything, just to get my own violin."

" A violin is going to cost a lot more than a new coat would," observed her mother. " But we'll see what we can do, Bets. I don't even know if we can find a good instrument that we can afford."

Jean gripped her hands together and tried to keep back her wish for a grand piano. But it came out anyway, and the best she could do with it was to keep the expression light.

" If heaven sends us a little inheritance of, say, a hundred thousand dollars," she said, " my grand piano gets the first emergency rating."

Mr. Burnaby stared at his second daughter. " Are we trying to negotiate a grand piano? " he asked. " When did this happen? "

" Oh, we've given up the idea," Jean tried to be very casual about it. " My teacher thought I ought to have a new piano at the same time that Betsy's teacher wanted her to have a new violin. Anyway — "

" Well, for heaven's sake, let's try to be realistic about things! " her father exploded. " Just tell your teacher I'm a professor at the university, and they don't pay grand piano salaries. What's wrong with the upright? "

" Nothing the tuner can't fix," said Jean. She wished she hadn't mentioned her dream. It took some of the satisfaction out of renunciation to have her father say so bluntly that there had never been any choice anyway.

"Looks as if I'd better get back to work on that history," Mr. Burnaby said, glancing at his wife. "I'd kind of like to have that grand piano myself, if I could see any way to handle it."

Her mouth hanging open, Jean stared at her father incredulously.

"No use being frustrated over things we can't have," he went on philosophically. "I'd like a yacht too — if anyone ever gave me three wishes — and a 150-horsepower red convertible." He leered at his wife, who shuddered, and all the family burst into shouts of laughter. Jean closed her mouth and determined to be philosophical too. But she didn't think it was going to work.

A week later Mrs. Burnaby reported that she had answered an advertisement in the local paper for a fine old violin that was offered, with bow and case, for one hundred and fifty dollars. She had found an instrument that the teacher agreed was a very fine value. However, it must be bought this week end, if they wanted to get it, for another offer had been made, and the owner was willing to hold it for them for two days only.

"I don't know what to do about it," Mrs. Burnaby said unhappily. "Miss Kimball says she can hardly teach on the rented instrument and that Betsy is losing time practicing on it. Mr. Ryan says they haven't got another. This is exactly what Miss Kimball wants her to have. And this is the month there isn't a cent to spare. One of the big insurance bills comes this week."

Mr. Burnaby got up slowly and put on the old single-speed record player one of his favorite records. Returning to his chair, he said with a touch of annoyance: "When I think of all the things we've never been able to get that we thought we needed — and now we've got to get a violin! Well, if you think Betsy is really serious about this business, Sara, I suppose we'll have to do something about the instrument. I'll just have to talk to the bank about a loan, I suppose."

"I wish there were some other way," said Mrs. Burnaby. "I hate to borrow money — it seems to take forever to pay it back."

Jean, working at the desk on a list of invitations that had to go out to her Y club, tried not to listen. But she found herself unable to concentrate on anything else. Money, money, money. Never enough, always a problem. This time she had the money. She was saving it for her own instrument, she tried to tell herself. But she thought of Sally giving up the formal dress she had counted on, to help out with Ricky's dog. Stealing a glance at her parents, she thought they both looked worried.

"If we could just wait till your book is finished and not have another loan," her mother said.

"I've got some money," Jean heard her own voice saying comfortingly. It gave her an unexpected warmth to be reassuring her parents. "I've got a couple of hundred dollars, Mom. I was saving it for college — or the grand piano, or some other emergency. But I'll get this violin for Betsy, and we can figure out the other emergency when it happens."

"Oh, honey," cried her mother. "We don't want to take your money. I know how much you want that piano."

Jean shrugged, with a fine effect of nonchalance.

"What I've got wouldn't be enough for the piano anyway," she said. "If we've got to buy a violin, let's get a good one when we can. Maybe the piano will wait." She

71

rose to go to her room and get her bankbook.

"Thank you very much, Jean," said her father. "That will be a great help." She heard her father say, as she went upstairs: "I don't like to use the kids' money, either, Sara. But the fact is, we've put a lot of money into Jean's music in the last six years. It's a generous gesture for her to help with Betsy's music now. And if we can help her get that piano — the main thing is for the family to help each other, as each need arises."

"One hundred dollars would be enough, Jean," he said, when she came down again. "I've got the other fifty. I'll meet you at the bank tomorow, and we can make the withdrawal."

Jean felt a warm glow of satisfaction in being able to be generous. But the glow faded when she had made the withdrawal the next afternoon and looked at her balance. Suddenly she remembered how long it had taken her to save that hundred dollars. She went on from the bank to her music lesson, thinking sadly of the piano that was going to be sold in February, the only make she wanted, and a value that she could probably not find again. It seemed bitter that music should be hedged about with such sacrifices.

Her faith was restored, astonishingly, within an hour. Miss Austin reported that Mrs. Turner had decided to keep the piano until June.

"She says two of her pupils are so exciting this year, they show so much promise, that she can't bear to break off her teaching in February," said Miss Austin, with a gleam of excitement in her own eyes at the good luck of a friend in having such pupils. "They begged her to work with them through the year. I thought she might not want to

72

leave even in June. But they must leave her then for the summer, and next year they go away to college. So she's retiring definitely in June — if you can get along without the piano for that long."

Jean felt as if she had received a last-minute reprieve from execution.

"That will be much better for us," she said quickly. "Dad didn't see how he could buy it very soon. But if we can wait till June something might turn up, and I just hated to see that piano go to someone else."

"I asked her about the price," Miss Austin went on, "and she said she knew it was worth a thousand dollars, but for a friend of mine with real musical promise she'd be willing to take eight hundred dollars. She's attached to the instrument — feels sentimental about it — and she'd like to know it was going to a musician. We'll go over and play on it so that you can get acquainted with her."

In the rebound from reluctant renunciation, Jean felt as if the piano were immediately within her grasp, and she wanted to dance and sing in her delight.

Even the old piano at home, when she returned from her lesson sounded better than she remembered.

"The tuner was here today," her mother said, when Jean remarked on its improved condition. "He says this is really a good upright."

"It's not bad at all," Jean said magnanimously. "Mrs. Turner doesn't want to sell her piano now until June, so the next immediate emergency is postponed."

"It just doesn't pay to worry," Mrs. Burnaby observed. "You know, I have a feeling that we'll get that piano. With more time to figure things out, maybe something will happen. And that reminds me " — what had reminded her was not clear, but Jean was used to her mother's some-times disconnected trains of thought — "if the Ballards have no plans for Thanksgiving, would you like to invite them here for the day? We have no other guests coming. Grandma is going to Uncle Tom's this year. And I should think spending Thanksgiving in a hotel would be dismal."

"That would be fine." Jean was pleased and touched at this thought for Kim, after all her mother's criticisms of her best friend.

"I'd like to know Mr. and Mrs. Ballard," said Mrs. Burnaby too casually. Jean grinned at her mother wick-edly, recognizing immediately the motive behind the invitation.

"I'll call Kim tonight," she said, "and you can talk to her mother then. I'm sure they're not planning anything else. Kim said something about sitting around the hotel all day long and she didn't look forward to it."

"They always seem to be going away for week ends," Mrs. Burnaby remarked. "I wonder how they happen not to be invited for Thanksgiving."

"Those friends have gone to Cuba to stay over Christmas," Jean told her. "And some other friends are going to Iowa to see their relatives. It's going to be fun having them here — I'll tell them about four, shall I?"

CHAPTER 7

JEAN had seen Mrs. Ballard only once, when she had happened to be at home the third time Kim had invited Jean to come up to the hotel room and do some homework. On all the other occasions when Jean had gone home with Kim, Mrs. Ballard had been working in a studio downtown, or lecturing to a class at the Art Institute, or appearing on the program of the Fine Arts Association. She had a very busy professional life, and Jean admired her greatly by reputation. Kim discussed her family as if they were three individuals who happened to be living together without making any demands upon each other or interfering with each other's lives. It sounded to Jean like an ideal arrangement. Kim made her own decisions, and her family never seemed to argue about her plans.

Kim was very co-operative, too, about always leaving a note for them, telling them where she was going. " Back about two A.M., but don't worry before three," she would say, when Jean and Jeff called for her to go to a dance. Then, since Jean usually had to be home by one, Kim would be home more often than not earlier than she had told her parents to expect her.

Jean was sure that when their parents were well acquainted everything about Kim would be better understood. Her own father and mother would see what unusual and interesting people Kim's parents were, and be pleased that she and Kim were such close friends.

Thanksgiving dinner was scheduled for 4:30 at the Burnabys. That meant that the turkey could be stuffed early in the morning and put in the oven before ten, without anyone having to rise with the dawn. Mr. Burnaby insisted that such a momentous dinner as the Thanksgiving feast deserved to begin earlier than the usual 6:30 hour they observed during the rest of the year.

Jean and Sally cut bread for stuffing, strung beans, peeled potatoes, prepared onions, set the table, Sally interested in learning the techniques of preparing a Thanksgiving dinner, Jean anxious that everything should be exactly right for the important guests. She arranged and rearranged the centerpiece of squash, gourds, red apples, and oranges, and a cluster of red grapes half a dozen times before she was satisfied. At 3:30 she discovered that the burned-down candles on the table had not been replaced, and there were no new ones in the house. Frantic, she took the car and rode out to look for a drugstore that might be open. It was 4:15 when she finally returned with four white candles she had located in a faraway store.

The Ballards had not yet arrived. Bob Carlson was talking to Mr. Burnaby, his eyes half shut, with the good-humored easy grin that gave an unexpected, impish expression to his face. Tall and blond and easygoing, Bob was a junior this year at Northern, where he was taking a premedical course and played fullback on the football team. He had been going with Sally since she had entered Northern a year ago. Since Christmas they had been together two or three nights a week, and Sally had gone with no one else. He was telling about one of the professors who liked to trap his students into errors, and then expose them to the laughter of the class. On this occasion, the student pretended to be stupidly falling into the trap, and then suddenly, with a well-phrased question, caught the professor in his own net. The class had laughed for ten minutes, and the professor, outraged, had stalked out of the room.

Mr. Burnaby laughed as heartily as the class had laughed, and Bob enjoyed the affair all over again.

"I wonder what's keeping our other guests," Mrs. Burnaby said, with a look at the clock. "Didn't you tell them around four, Jean?"

"I said four," affirmed Jean. "Kim said they wouldn't be doing anything — "

Mrs. Burnaby raised one eyebrow. "We'll eat as soon as they get here, but I thought it would be nice to visit for a couple of minutes before we sat down."

Jean checked the preparations again: cranberry sauce glowed in a low glass bowl, rolls were fragrant in the oven, butter was cut for the table, salad was mixed in a wooden bowl. Mince and pumpkin pies waited on the counter in the kitchen, the vegetables were cooked. How long could you keep potatoes that were ready to mash and beans ready to drain and butter?

The doorbell rang, and Jean's tight nerves jumped. She hurried back to the front hall, just as Jimmy reached the door. Her mother cut off her remark to Bob and started across the living room.

"Jean!" yelled Jimmy, holding the door open, "Here's your friends!"

Embarrassed and wanting to shake him for such manners, Jean greeted the Ballards. "Do come in," she said. "I'm so glad you could come."

Mrs. Burnaby reached the door almost at the same time.

"Mother," said Jean, "this is Mrs. Ballard and Mr. Ballard. You know Kim, of course."

Mrs. Ballard was thin and angular, with heavy black hair, cut in a thick bang across her forehead, and exotic earrings. She spoke to her hostess as if she had known her all her life, confiding to Mrs. Burnaby her anger over something that had happened at the hotel as if she knew Mrs. Burnaby would understand how difficult things could be.

Mr. Ballard, thickset and tall, with heavy hair still blond, wore a baggy tweed suit and a very loud tie.

They met Mr. Burnaby and Bob Carlson and all the rest of the family, who by now were sitting around in a circle waiting for something to happen.

"Which is the little girl who plays the violin?" Mrs. Ballard asked in a deep voice. "Betsy? Ah!"

She stared at Betsy intently while she fitted a cigarette into a very long ivory holder.

Then she said to Mrs. Burnaby: "Very interesting face, hasn't she? I'd love to do that face—"

Her mother looked nonplused for the first time that Jean could remember. Then she said: "Has she? I never noticed."

Mrs. Ballard leaned toward her as if she had found a soul mate.

"You never recognize it in your own children. I remember when Gabriel told me Kim was photogenic and he wanted her to model for him. I was astounded! Then of

78

course, when I studied her face I could see exactly what he meant. You see those planes through the cheeks? And the way the nose joins the cheeks?"

Kim said to Jean: "Let's go out in the kitchen. I love your house — " and the girls escaped. Jean could recognize Mrs. Ballard's maternal instinct operating exactly like Mrs. Burnaby's, and she felt a rush of sympathy for her friend.

Mrs. Burnaby joined them within a few minutes, directing the tossing of the salad, placing vegetables on the table, setting the turkey before Mr. Burnaby's place, with the sharp knife and the long fork.

It seemed incredible that everyone should be so congenial when they sat about the Burnaby table. The Ballards talked as easily and intimately as if they had known the Burnabys all their lives. The meal was almost over before Jean realized that almost no one had talked except the Ballards.

Mr. Burnaby said: "What do you think about this Korean situation, Mr. Ballard? Bob here would be glad to know what to expect in that direction."

"Well, if you want to know what I think," Mr. Ballard sounded pontifical, as if he were accustomed to being consulted on matters of state importance, "we're involved in a big thing over there, and it takes the most delicate handling. There's no telling just now which way the cat is going to jump, and we've got to be prepared for anything. Now one place the State Department made a big mistake — "

He went on for several minutes, and it all sounded fascinating and important to Jean. Mrs. Ballard also had opinions about foreign affairs which seemed to accord with her husband's.

"Of course, when we were over there," she offered, during a pause, "I was fascinated with the North Koreans. Most wonderful faces — broad planes, lowering, brooding eyebrows. Stark, brute endurance. I wanted to model them the minute I saw them."

"Those were the South Koreans," her husband corrected her. "We were in Seoul for a couple of weeks," he turned to the Burnabys and outlined the itinerary they had followed on assignment before arriving in Berlin.

Kim whispered to Jean: "Mother gets so excited about stark brute primitives. I didn't like any of them, except one of the officers who was worried about his family. I was glad to get to Berlin."

"You remember that time in Indo-China?" Mrs. Ballard turned to Kim and went on with an anecdote about revolution which had aroused in her a mad desire to model everyone in sight.

"Paris I rejected," she said, waving the ivory holder with an expression of fatigue. "It no longer has anything to offer the artist. Now here in Chicago there is more of the brute primitive than there is in Paris. I *love* Chicago. But of course I'll want to go on at the end of the year. I always want to go on."

The younger Burnabys were beginning to get bored with the adult conversation in which there was no place for them. The girls cleared the table. Mrs. Burnaby suggested that the smaller children should be served at once so that they could be excused, and Ricky, Betsy, and Jimmy disappeared upstairs.

"How do you like Sherwood?" Mrs. Burnaby asked. "Jean says your husband went to our high school."

"It's delightful," said Mrs. Ballard. "So typically suburban. Just the sort of thing you read about, but suburban life has been outside our experience before this year. Kim loves it. But it's quite a change from Paris, isn't it, darling?"

Kim shrugged in a very French way.

"I'm happy enough not to have a *bonne* running around with me everywhere I go," she said, laughing lightly. To Jean she said: "You know, in Paris no well brought up young lady goes out on the street alone. I used to sneak out when no one was looking, and the other ladies on the street — Oo, la, la! They were shocked! Men would whistle and offer to take me home."

Her mother smiled tolerantly as if the caprices of youth were amusing.

"Kim is so independent," she observed. "We've brought her up to be independent and self-reliant, of course. But it was hard for the French to get used to her, or for her to get used to the French. This was a good time for her to be in America."

"She seems to have fitted into an American high school as if she were used to it," Mrs. Burnaby said.

"She is so fond of Jean," said Mrs. Ballard. To Jean she said, turning to her confidentially: "You may not know how much we count on you, Jean. We could never feel so confident and happy about Kim if we didn't know she was with you most of the time."

Startled, Jean looked down and stirred her coffee busily, trying to think of an answer.

"Kim and I have a good time together," she said at last, feeling that it was a weak reply.

"I'm sure you must," agreed Mrs. Ballard. "We just feel it was the luckiest thing in our assignment here that Kim found someone she likes so much, who has so much in common with her, and who will be with her the way you are. It's a lonely life for her, in the hotel, you know, and when you are with her, we know we don't have to worry."

She turned back to Mrs. Burnaby, who was looking a little incredulous at this acclaim for her daughter, and went on rapidly about how busy she herself was in getting ready for a show in an art gallery on Michigan Avenue that specialized in modern work.

Sally and Bob began to do the dishes, while Jean and Kim cleared the table. Mrs. Burnaby asked Kim to play for them, and without too much hesitation Kim agreed. Betsy came downstairs and offered Kim her new violin with great pride. She was suffused with delight when Kim picked it up carefully and said, " That's a very fine instrument, Betsy."

" She plays beautifully," said Mrs. Burnaby, when Kim had finished the selection on which she and Jean had been working. She sounded surprised, as if, in spite of all she had heard about Kim, she found it hard to believe she could play so well. " I think you must have a very talented daughter, Mrs. Ballard."

"Yes, she has talent," Mrs. Ballard agreed, leaning forward to smash out her cigarette in the ash tray. " She could do anything. Her trouble is to choose one thing and settle down to it. I'd like to see her paint myself. The one thing we are not interested in her doing is the stage. But we'll see."

Loosening the bow and returning the instrument to its case, Kim made a face at Jean.

" I don't know why Mother takes this attitude about the stage," she muttered. " Anything else would be all right.

But theater is a blind spot with her. We just don't discuss it any more."

The dishes were done and Sally and Bob made their farewells as they went out to see some friends. The Ballards glanced at the clock in astonishment that it could be 8:30 already, and made preparations to depart.

"I've got to run downtown with an article for tomorrow's paper before 10:30," said Mr. Ballard, putting on his coat. "Our evenings are always short with that deadline hanging over my head every night."

"We're so glad you could be with us," Mrs. Burnaby said.

Mrs. Ballard threw a rich fur casually about her shoulders. She smiled as she said good-by. "Take care of my little girl," she said, as if it were a quip, and Jean thought, watching her, that her smile had in it no humor, no tenderness, only a kind of mordant wit that might be uncomfortable to live with. She was undecided about her feeling for Mrs. Ballard now, the sculptress was so different from any mother or teacher she had known. She was, to say the least, a very "interesting" person. Jean could see Kim becoming like her mother as she grew older and harder and more cynical.

Her own father and mother said very little about their guests, whether to spare Jean's feelings, or because they themselves were baffled by these cosmopolitan personalities.

On looking back, the thing that Jean remembered most vividly of that day was Mrs. Ballard's final charge to her, "Take care of my little girl." She felt inescapably as if she had been assigned a big responsibility.

CHAPTER 8

JEAN did not see much of Kim outside of school for a week after Thanksgiving. Her music these days was taking more and more time, and in turn that tightened up her study hours, so that for days together she spent no time walking in to the center of town to shop or sitting over a Coke to chat about school and friends.

Her music teacher was planning to present Jean in a solo recital in the spring, to which the members of the scholarship committee of Overton College would be invited. Overton had a noted department of music.

"You have a very good chance of getting a musical scholarship," Miss Austin said, with that look of excitement that at once warmed Jean and worried her. "You might get one for Northern University if you want to stay at home next year."

"I'd *love* to get away," said Jean intensely. "I hadn't thought much about it, because I knew the folks couldn't afford to send Sally away. Would a scholarship be enough so it wouldn't cost any more to go to Overton than to stay home?"

"Some scholarships are very good," said Miss Austin.

"I'm not sure how much the different ones offer. But I think at least two pay tuition and private lessons. Of course, they are offered on a regional basis — you would be competing against entries all through the Middle West. But I really believe you've got a good chance, Jean, if you work hard from now to May as you have since last summer. You're becoming a very fine pianist."

Trudging home through the deep snow, Jean felt very mature and adult about her music. She knew that since last summer she had discovered a new satisfaction in mastering finger techniques, that she enjoyed working at scales for an hour at a time, increasing her dexterity and working up to faster and faster tempos without losing the smooth, even touch her teacher wanted. It had become almost like a game, like improving her diving form, or her tennis form, when she was a sophomore. Only the satisfactions were deeper and richer when she could recognize her own improvement on the piano. She tried to tell herself that the old piano was no handicap!

But she had played on Mrs. Turner's piano and discovered a response and a richness of tone in the instrument that she had never experienced before. She had fallen in love with it immediately. Now Miss Austin urged her to try to practice at her studio a couple of times a week, in order to work on the grand piano there, and when Jean remembered Mrs. Turner's piano just waiting for her to claim it — and pay for it — her heart turned over and sank.

During that week of concentration she had not even seen Jeff outside of school. He called her daily, immediately after supper, and talked about things they could do over the week end. He himself was on the swimming squad, and that kept him as busy as Jean.

By the time the Christmas activities at the high school required afterschool rehearsals, she had cleared away other requirements, and managed to practice, study, shop, rehearse, in a co-ordinated pattern where nothing got left out and nothing seemed to crowd too much. For two weeks she lived on a high level of competence and satisfaction. She wondered if this was what it was like to be grown-up: to be able to handle everything you had to do with no conflicts and almost no mistakes, pleasing yourself as well as everyone you worked with. It was wonderful while it lasted. Jean tried to tell herself there was no reason why life shouldn't go on like this, but she knew, subconsciously, that sooner or later something was going to snap.

Everyone at school was making plans for the Nightingales' Christmas Carnival, held at the Shoreline Country Club midweek between Christmas and New Year. Jean had gone last year, as a Nightingale, with a boy she had hardly liked. Jeff had gone with another girl, and Jean had been miserable when she had seen him. She wondered if she wanted to go this year, as an outsider, and with Jeff.

When he asked her to go, she decided quickly that she would like it, just to wipe out the memory of last year's unsatisfactory party. Perhaps she would even wear the same gown, the holly-red taffeta that was the only thing she had enjoyed about the occasion. Then she put the date out of her mind. The student body were looking forward to the pre-Christmas party on Friday night, and for that party Jean and Jeff were double dating with Kim and Tony.

It had been several weeks since they had had a double

date, and when Kim mentioned it to Jean, Jean had suggested that Kim should have Tony arrange it with Jeff. So it was arranged, and although Jean had spent days planning how to reply if Jeff made any gloomy objections to it, she was pleased to find that he seemed to think this party might be fun.

Kim's father had bought a second car in the fall, since he used one for his work all the time, and Mrs. Ballard and Kim shared the new blue Victoria. But it seemed to be available for Kim so much that she called it " my car," to the envy of her three friends. It was extremely handy to have a car in the crowd which was always available, and whenever they double dated, it was in Kim's car. And Kim was so generous about letting the boys drive that they enjoyed it as much as she did.

Jeff and Jean had been waiting half an hour when the blue car swept around the corner of Juniper Lane with a screech and a squawk of the horn, and squealed to a fast stop before the house.

Mr. Burnaby looked up from his professional journal and said ominously, " I don't know why they don't include manners in the drivers' training course out at that high school."

" O Dad," said Jean patiently, " Tony knows all those things. This is just a kind of joke. You know — youth's high spirits."

" Well," he conceded, " just so he doesn't try any funny business out in traffic."

" He's an expert driver," his daughter assured him. " Tony's been driving the Latimers' car for three years now, and he's never scratched a fender. A little noise doesn't hurt anyone."

"Don't worry, Mr. Burnaby," said Jeff. "If I think Tony is feeling irresponsible tonight, I'll take the wheel myself."

"Of course, it's only Kim's car," observed Jean. "She never gets a chance at it when the boys are along."

"Just get back safe," said her father. "What time?"

"Oh, the usual time," said Jean vaguely. "The dance is over at 12:30 and we always have to eat. 1:30?"

"Seeing this is the kickoff for vacation, 1:30," her father agreed, with a half-smile.

The white snow creaked underfoot as they walked out to the waiting car. Overhead the bare branches were dark against a moonlit sky. The cold air was fresh against their cheeks, and Jean's spirits soared on a gust of enthusiasm. School was out, studies were past, tonight was a time to play.

They had never made such hilarious foolery. Jeff kept making droll observations on life and love that seemed to spark answering witicisms from everyone. Tony's clowning was hysterically funny. Even Jeff, pretending to be above such nonsense, collapsed into helpless laughter. Kim was at the top of her form, sparkling and dynamic, and Jean thought how lucky she was to have such friends.

The gym was decorated like Santa Claus's castle, glittering with snow and icicles. Jeff, on the dance floor, flung Jean about in an apache rhythm that drew an admiring circle and applause. Jean was nonplused. Jeff had never been so recklessly abandoned when he danced. A smooth and expert dancer, usually he danced quietly and unobtrusively. But tonight he seemed to have cast aside his reticence and inhibitions. Tonight he was frankly having fun, and Jean kept up with him. She liked him in this mood most of all.

88

They traded dances, and Tony confided to Jean that he'd never seen old Jeff come out of his shell like this. He implied that it came from Jeff's devotion to Jean, and the fact that she'd been nice to him lately, and Jean had an uneasy sense of being given credit for something she had never done, and yet could not say so. Then the talk shifted to Kim.

At 11:30 the four of them stood near the door during an intermission and watched the other dancers.

Suddenly Kim said, snapping her fingers: "I've got a wonderful idea, kids. We've danced long enough. Let's go out to the Gypsy Tearoom and get our fortunes told!"

"Oh, let's!" exclaimed Jean, fired with the idea of hearing her fortune.

The boys looked at each other. "Fortunetelling!" said Jeff, with a snort. "You mean you believe that nonsense?"

"Certainly I don't *believe* it," cried Kim. "If it were serious, it would be terrifying. An old gypsy told me in Paris two years ago that I was coming to America soon — and that was long before Dad got the Chicago assignment. So?"

Tony said suddenly: "I always get a kick out of fortunetelling. How much is this going to set us back? Have we got enough with us?"

Jean wished it hadn't come up, having no idea how much it would cost, nor how much Jeff had with him.

But Kim said: "Oh, it costs hardly anything! We can drink coffee, and the fortuneteller will come around and read our palms for a dollar apiece. I'll pay for all of us!"

"Aw, you will not!" both boys said together. "We've got plenty of money. O.K. — let's get going."

Jean had had her fortune told years ago at a carnival,

where someone had read her handwriting and told her that she was introspective, artistic, talented, and so forth. She could no longer remember how much was true and what had been disproved.

"Don't you really think it's fun, Jeff? " she said, as they drove over to the Gypsy Tearoom, on a highway outside of town. "I simply love fortunetelling."

He looked at her oddly, as if he were going to disagree and then changed his mind.

"I guess it's fun," he conceded. "Only the idea of anyone paying any attention to that nonsense always makes me kind of mad. Maybe I take the scientific approach to things."

They talked about hunches and odd phenomena which science had never been able to prove or disprove, and by the time they parked near the Gypsy Tearoom Jean felt that Jeff was entering into this game with all the zest with which he would approach a scientific experiment.

"We're lucky we're early," observed Kim, looking about the half-empty tearoom. It was a low-ceilinged, dimly lighted room, with waitresses in peasant costume, and the minor sound of a gypsy violin somewhere in the shadows. "I heard some of the other kids at the dance saying they were coming here later. This place will be mobbed in another hour."

They ordered coffee and doughnuts and asked for the fortuneteller, who was busy with three customers ahead of them. Over the coffee they talked about next year's plans, careers, travel, colleges, fellowships. Jeff wanted to take a hostel trip, which none of the others had thought of, and that brought on an animated discussion. Jean felt closer to Jeff than she had since last fall.

The gypsy arrived at their table in a varicolored, long-skirted costume, with strings of beads and earrings that pierced her ears. Jean studied her with interest, wondering if she were real or made up. She had a strong, dark, foreign face, a dour expression, and she kept her eyes cast down as if she did not care to see their faces. She could be Hungarian, Jean decided. She looked authentic. She read palms and tea leaves, but since they had not ordered tea, she would read their palms only.

"I never could feel any faith in tea leaves," Jean whispered to Jeff, as she held out her hand to the gypsy.

Clutching her hand tight, the gypsy looked once at Jean's face with shrewd black eyes, and then began to talk. She told Jean she was musical, that she had a talented sister, was going to get a lot of money, and had not yet found her true love. Jean found herself listening with greater credulity than she had believed she had. Something in the woman's face and manner was very convincing. And all that about the talented sister — how could she have known? They had not even mentioned Betsy tonight. And the money. She wanted to ask how much it would be — the music scholarship? or the grand piano? But the gypsy refused to answer questions. She dropped Jean's hand and picked up Kim's outthrust palm.

Jean tried to listen, but her own predictions kept going around in her mind so that it was hard to hear anything else. In the dim, smoky room, where the only light came from candles guttering on the tables and a shaded sconce in each of the four corners, suddenly an eerie conviction of foresight came over Jean.

She looked at Jeff, about to say something to him, and found him staring at the gypsy gloomily. Suddenly he looked at Jean and away again. He had declared earlier that the girls could listen to that nonsense if they wanted to, but not for him. Now, as she finished reading Tony's palm, he thrust out his own hand and said, "Let's hear the worst."

Ignoring this challenge to smile, the gypsy leaned over his hand and muttered: "Very interesting. Very good. I see big success, big travel, and big heartbreak. You have an interest in science, where you will go far. But you should believe what I say in spite of your science, because I can read it here. You are going to be unhappy. Very unhappy. But it will pass. Everything passes."

With that philosophic reassurance, she accepted her money from the boys and went on to another table. Jean dreamed a moment, staring into the smoke rings floating about the other tables, thinking of the things she had hoped to hear. Success, money, talent. Everything she hoped for was going to happen. What a delightful thing to believe!

She glanced at Jeff. "What do you think now?" she dared him. "I liked what I heard."

He shrugged. "I'm going to be unhappy and you haven't found your true love. Is that what you wanted to hear?"

"But you don't believe those things!"

"But you do!"

She felt as if her secret uneasiness about Jeff's caring too much for her had been dragged into the open and exposed to daylight, secrets that she had never, never wanted him to know. What could she say?"

She tried to be light and reassuring at the same time. "Oh, you know, Jeff — you believe what you want and discard what you want, in these things. You never worry about unhappiness — "

"Either you believe all of it, or none of it," he said flatly. "You can't pick and choose."

Jean stared at the flickering candle again, trying to say something cheerful. She couldn't shake the feeling that had come over her of truth in the gypsy's soothsaying, she couldn't tell Jeff that it was all true after all, and she had not found her true love. But she wished he hadn't heard that part of it. In spite of the glamorous promise of success, she wished now that they hadn't come here. Jeff was upset, although he tried not to show it. Across the table Kim and Tony were having a serious discussion about their prophecies. Jean looked at her watch.

"Come on, kids," she got to her feet. "It's one o'clock, and time to be leaving. I've got to be in by 1:30 tonight."

"I'd just as soon leave this house of doom," Jeff said, holding her coat. "That's what I have against these fortunetellers. Always full of sorrow and woe."

"You know perfectly well that's the only reason you believe in them at all," Kim teased him. "If they predicted nothing but sunshine and success, you'd scorn them entirely. Now that she's told you a little rain will fall into your life, you're all in a tizzy."

"Not me," denied Jeff stoutly. "I don't believe a word of any of it. Success in science, hah! I'm going hosteling someday, and maybe I'll wind up a tramp. What's she going to think then?"

The clear, cold white-framed night was fresh and stimulating when they came out of the smoky tearoom into the parking lot. Jean drew a tingling breath of the frosty air and felt better. She slipped her arm through Jeff's.

"Don't be unhappy just yet," she whispered. "Maybe

fate will forget you after all."

He grinned and patted her hand as they climbed into the car. But she knew that underneath his nonchalance he was less secure than he had been before the gypsy had read their palms.

Drat her, Jean thought, as the car backed around to face the highway, she must have been better than I thought —

A long, wailing siren howled down the highway toward them. Jean's nerves jumped at the sound, and before she could speak three fire engines sped past.

"Oh, a fire!" cried Kim. "Tony, follow them! Hurry!"

Tony turned into the highway after the engines, and Kim leaned over the back of the seat to face Jeff and Jean.

"I can't resist a fire," she said, her eyes sparkling with excitment. "It's one of my compulsions. Isn't this a perfect finale for the evening?"

"I've got to get home," Jean protested without conviction. "Where is the fire?"

"They're turning off the highway right ahead," Kim assured her, glancing through the windshield. "This won't take more than five minutes. You know how fires are — they're usually out before you even get there. We're in luck tonight."

Tony slowed down and stopped at the edge of the road.

"That's a narrow road in there," he said, flashing the spotlight on it. "I don't know about getting in there, in all this snow —"

"Oh, go ahead," Kim ordered impatiently. "I'll take the wheel if you're nervous, Tony. I could take this little car anywhere. Besides, the engines have beaten a track. Come on — you can't sit here on the highway!"

Tony turned, without further protest, into the narrow lane, deeply rutted with snow, where the engines had turned.

"I'm not sure this is such a good idea," he was saying to himself. "But whose party is it, anyway?"

"I like the pioneer spirit," Kim told him. "You're doing fine, boy. Just keep going."

Torn between excitement, as they approached the burning house, worry about her deadline for getting in, and an invincible reluctance to spoil somebody else's fun, Jean looked questioningly at Jeff.

"Can we make it?" she murmured.

To her astonishment Jeff's eyes were shining with excitement.

"Oh, sure," he said. "It's only ten minutes to get home from here."

They pulled up at a small clearing filled with other cars and a police ambulance. A barricade prevented them from moving out of the lane.

Before them a large country house was burning, with flames breaking through the roof and a crowd of frantic people running about in the snow. From the second-story window a child was being handed down to a fireman on a ladder. Jean's blood froze, as she suddenly realized what a fire really meant.

"You don't think anyone is going to be — caught in there, do you?" She leaned close to Jeff for comfort. He put his arm about her and held her tight.

"Don't worry, honey," he said, and the endearment was comforting. "The firemen are right on the job. Look — there comes a piece of furniture out of the window."

A fireman on the roof was directing a stream of water.

Jean looked from him to the shivering people in the snow, wrapped in blankets.

" I'll find out how it started," Tony said, climbing out of the car. They watched him approach the policeman guarding the space around the building, who talked to him for several minutes.

"Defective wiring in the third floor," Tony reported, returning after some minutes. " Fire broke out in a room full of old papers, and nobody knew it till it burned through a second-floor ceiling. Nearest neighbors are around a bend in the road and at this time of night nobody noticed anything. Everybody's out — nobody hurt, neighbors are taking the family in for the night. In fact, everybody is on the way to bed right this minute."

Jean sighed with relief, and some of the hilarious spirit of the earlier evening revived in all of them.

" Maybe we'd better get on our way," she suggested.

Kim grinned at her over the back seat, dimple challenging.

" Even I am ready to leave," she said. " Best fire I ever saw: old firetrap burned down but insured (we hope), nobody hurt, valuable antiques saved, everyone cared for — what more could you ask in a fire, besides three engines? "

Tony started the motor.

"What's the best way out of here? " he asked Jeff. " Are we clear behind? "

Jeff turned his head. " There's a bend in the road, but take it slow, and I'll tell you when to turn."

" I can't see a thing," Tony observed, wrestling with the wheel. " Between a one-track road full of hedges and curves, and no back-up lights on your car, Miss Ballard, we're lucky if we get out of here."

"I'll get those back-up lights before the next fire," Kim promised.

"Hold it!" exclaimed Jeff. They had moved about fifty feet. "There's a car here without lights. Now who belongs to that, do you suppose?"

"Can't I get around it?"

"Fence on one side," Jeff reported, "and you can't take a chance on the other side — looks like a ditch full of snow."

"I'll go back where we came from," Tony said, considering. "Maybe I can turn around or something up near the house."

They moved forward fifty feet and stopped.

"This deep snow is getting mushy," Tony said. "If we scramble around in it much more, we'll be in real trouble."

He got out of the car and reconnoitered, returning to report: "Boys and girls, it doesn't look good. The engines are blocking the exit and they don't look in a mood to move the engines. In fact, they can't move while they've got the hoses connected."

"Goody, we can wait till the end of the show," cried Kim.

Jean was thinking hard. It was after 1:30 now, she was already late, and there was obviously no way to telephone.

"Can you think of anything, Jeff?" she looked up at him. "Do we have to sit here all night?"

"I'll see what I can find out." Jeff left the car in his turn, and Jean felt a reassuring confidence in his ability to find an answer to any problem. He moved among the firemen and policemen, talking first to one and then to another.

"Guess we'll have to sit it out," he reported cheerfully when he returned. "Firemen say this is a tricky blaze, keeps breaking out in different spots. They can't leave till they know it's out. Police are sympathetic, but can't do a thing about us. The car behind is stuck in the snow. The owner came over from down the way, tried to back out, and finally left it and walked home."

"Hah! " Tony guffawed, and accidentally hit the horn ring. Jean jumped at the blast. "How about a little night music? " He switched on the radio. "Hey, look, there's another blaze, over in the far corner of the roof."

Only Jean was really disturbed by this contretemps. She kept thinking of her father, probably pacing the floor worrying. She knew what he would say when she came in. Deeper than her dislike of his scolding was her real concern for his worry. She wished there were some way to let him know what had happened. She knew Jeff felt the same way she did — concerned for both her parents and his own, yet knowing there was no use fussing about it before the others.

If Tony were concerned at all, he was concealing it very well. And Kim was openly excited about this development. Her eyes sparkled, as she described getting taken into custody by the Reds in Berlin, when it took her parents and the United States consul four hours to get her released.

"Do you specialize in catastrophe? " Jeff asked.

Kim laughed, and her eyes flashed.

"I don't know why it is," she said, "but the most exciting things seem to happen to me, and I just love it. I wasn't worried, that time in Berlin. I knew it would come out all right. But you'd think I'd jeopardized the fate of the United Nations, the way the consul carried on, when he got me back in West Berlin. And I'd only gone across the line a quarter of a mile — just for the fun of it."

They began exchanging stories about narrow escapes and daring adventures. The motor was turned off to save gas and battery, and it was growing cold in the car. Jean huddled against Jeff trying to keep warm. Already the excitement of being trapped had worn off, and boredom was setting in. She yawned helplessly, wondering if it would be any fun to climb out in the snow and have a moonlight snow fight. But they were not dressed for scuffling in the snow, and Jean felt tired at the idea. All she wanted now was to get home and into a warm bed.

At 2:30 the engines pulled away from the blackened, dripping house. Tony followed the engines, and they found themselves back on the highway. At quarter to three they stopped in front of Jean's house, where the living room was brightly lighted. She could see her father walk away from the window, as they stopped.

"Don't wait for me," said Jeff to Tony, as he got out of the car with Jean. "I only live three blocks from here, and I'm going in and see Jean's father."

It was good of Jeff to be so concerned, Jean thought, as she walked up the steps with him. He was sweet, and he had been fun tonight. And she was so tired she could hardly think.

"I'm terribly sorry about this, Mr. Burnaby," said Jeff, without visibly quailing. He was very courageous, Jean thought. Her father was extremely angry, she knew, and braver boys than Jeff might have preferred not to face him.

"Thanks for coming in and telling me the whole story."

Mr. Burnaby shook hands with Jeff when the story was told. "I can see it wasn't your fault. But it sounds like a kind of wild-eyed idea, to me, to turn into a single-lane country road, with this kind of snow. Didn't any one of you realize there'd be cars behind you, and you might be stuck?"

"No, sir, I guess we're just stupid," said Jeff disarmingly.

Mr. Burnaby suppressed an involuntary smile.

"O.K. — just don't do it again," he said. "I might say, Jeff, when Jean is with you I always feel as if she's being taken good care of. But times like this you think of accidents and everything."

"I know, sir," said Jeff apologetically. "My folks do too. O.K., Jean — see you next week —"

He ran down the street, sliding now and then on slick spots.

"Well, good night," said Jean to her parents. "I'm sorry you were worried. I knew you would be, but I couldn't do a thing."

"I know you don't do these things on purpose," said her mother, looking tired. "What I don't like is that they always seem to happen when you're out with Kim."

Jean tried to defend her friend. "That isn't fair, either, Mother. This wasn't any more Kim's fault than Tony's. It was just one of those things that looks good and then turns out complicated —"

Her mother looked unconvinced, and as Jean stumbled exhaustedly up to bed, she tried to tell herself that Kim was a victim of appearances. She couldn't help it if things like this just seemed to happen this year.

But she was too tired to make it stick.

CHAPTER 9

THE next day, Saturday, Jean began work at Vera Vaughan's candy store, where she nad worked during holidays for the past year. She had progressed from cupping chocolates last Christmas to selling behind the counter this year, since she knew the assortments of candy, and during the week before Christmas the customers stood two deep all along the counter.

Her hours were from noon to nine at night, with an hour for supper, and by nine Jean was exhausted. Jeff called to take her home, stopping for refreshment and conversation at the drug store on the way. He was working himself in the toy department of King's department store, where he ran the electric trains all day long.

Jeff was terribly sweet, Jean thought gratefully. He was concerned over her working so hard, and she appreciated it so much she thought she must be falling in love with him.

For weeks she had been giving thought to a Christmas present for him that he would especially like, and finally she chose an expensive book about planets and interstellar space, with beautiful color plates, that he had admired once when they saw it together in a bookstore window.

Her Christmas shopping was almost finished. She had only to find a present for Miss Austin, and she had discovered exactly what she wanted on her way to work Saturday morning: a copper pendant on a chain, with a design applied on it of a staff and two scattered notes. Jean was enchanted and wished she could have one for herself. But even if she couldn't afford to buy it for herself, she got a great deal of pleasure out of giving to someone else something she liked so much. She wished she could have felt the same pleasure in the present she had chosen for Jeff. Men, she decided, were hard to buy presents for. She wondered what Sally was getting Bob.

Thinking of Sally and Bob and Christmas, reminded her of Scotty. He would be coming home any day, and remembering him from last Christmas and last summer, she felt a thrill of anticipation.

Scotty was the boy next door, whom the Burnabys had known since he and Sally had been in kindergarten together. Two years ago, when Sally was a senior, she and Scotty had been pinned for the space of one short summer. They had even thought for a few hectic weeks that they wanted to get married immediately. But somehow — Jean never knew quite what had happened — they had changed their minds. Bob had come along, Scotty had gone away to school — and last Christmas Jean had suddenly understood what Sally had liked about Scotty. Only she knew, too, that to Scotty she was still Sally's little sister. She wondered if she would seem any older this year. Right that moment she was too tired to care. She fell asleep thinking how wonderful Sunday would be. No work.

Sunday afternoon Kim dropped in to leave a gift for

Jean and say good-by for the holidays. She was going to Mexico for two weeks with her parents.

"Mother is collecting Christmases," she said, as if it were an amusing hobby that anyone could pursue who happened to think of it. "She has a Japanese one, a German one, a French one, and an English one. She says she can't miss a Mexican Christmas, when she's so close to Mexico, and, besides, she wants to get away for a while."

"It sounds like a very original idea," said Jean, wishing she could travel the way the Ballards did. She looked at the decorations in their living room, the same ones the Burnabys used every year, and felt dull and unoriginal at the thought of Christmas repeating itself endlessly.

"Oh, it's all right," said Kim without enthusiasm. "Someday I think it would be fun to have a real American Christmas. But of course this year we couldn't do much in a hotel anyway."

The bell rang, and Jean got to her feet. During the holidays someone dropped in every day.

"Why, Scotty!"

He stood in the door, grinning at her with that wide, home-coming grin, and she thought swiftly: He gets better-looking all the time. "Do come in! We're terribly glad to see you!"

Red-haired and stocky, he walked into the living room with a springy motion, his head held high, and dropped his jacket on a chair.

"How's the family?" he wanted to know.

"They're all just fine. Mother will be here in a minute. She's finding Christmas decorations in the attic right now. Kim, I want to introduce a friend of mine — George Stephenson Scott — Scotty to his friends."

103

He stood before Kim and bowed slightly. There was a new suavity in his manner that Jean had never noticed before, and it gave him distinction. Does that come from being a sophomore? she wondered.

He threw himself down on the couch beside Kim and looked at home. Kim smiled at him, and her dimple was deeper than ever.

"Jean said you went to Colorado," she said. "Did you ever meet a boy named Rush Trent?"

"Rush? Say, do you know him? Great guy, isn't he?" Scotty sat up and began to talk about Rush, who had been in Paris one summer when Kim had been there. Rush was a pianist who had built up a popular dance band out at Colorado University.

"Did he ever tell you how Kim plays?" Jean asked.

Scotty looked at Kim with interest. "Do you play?"

"You should hear her," Jean bragged. "She's terrific on a fiddle."

"No fooling? Say, how's Betsy getting along? I hear from Mother that she's got talent."

"We're all cluttered up with talent this year," Jean said. "O Kim, do you have to go so soon?"

Kim had her coat wrapped about her, and she tied on a tiny hat with a wide veil. Through the veil she looked demure and glamorous.

"Say hello to Rush for me, will you?" she held out her hand to Scotty. "Maybe I'll see you again sometime, when we get back from Mexico."

When she was gone, Scotty said to Jean: "She looks like a girl I used to know at Colorado. I wonder if the resemblance will go any farther."

"What was the other girl like?"

"Oh, kind of cute and dashing," he said vaguely. "She was going to marry one of the boys in our house — went home last summer to make arrangements for a wedding in July, and then broke up the whole thing two weeks later. I didn't like her much."

"Well —" Jean wasn't sure what to say. The comparison didn't sound flattering. "You liked Kim, didn't you?"

"Oh, sure. Cute kid. I'm coming back here in February, transferring to Northern. Did your folks tell you?"

"No! Oh, that will be wonderful!"

He smiled at her, pleased with her enthusiasm. "Mother hasn't been any too well this fall, and she thinks she'd like me at home. Maybe I'll see more of you and your friend after that —"

Jean wondered how much he really liked Kim. "What about that girl we met you with last June at the movies — what was her name?"

"Oh, Ginny Whitaker! That broke up last summer. She's engaged to some guy in the Army, and I'm not going with anyone just now. I guess no one ever came up to the Burnaby girls!"

They both laughed at that. Scotty asked about Jeff and about Sally and Bob. When Jeff came in to take Jean to a Christmas program at the church, Scotty said, "Well, I'll be seeing you again — probably Christmas Day."

To Jeff he said, "You know this house is like my other home. I'm not really back from school until I've dropped in at the Burnabys'."

"Swell seeing you," said Jeff cordially. "Maybe we can get together sometime after Christmas is past."

"The nice thing about Christmas," Jean said, as they slid on the snow going out to the car, "is that you can stop and look back at the things you like to remember from other years. I'm just as glad Kim is away for a couple of weeks."

The week before Christmas passed quickly, as it does when time is crowded, and Christmas Eve was upon the n before Jean was ready for it after all.

She had not seen Scotty again, after his Sunday visit. But at eight o'clock on Christmas Eve he came over, happily casual, visiting with all the Burnabys as if he belonged there. Sally and Bob greeted him like an old friend and sat around and chatted for a while. Then they left, to drive up the shore and look at the lighted outdoor Christmas trees that decorated houses and grounds.

Jeff came in around 8:30, and Scotty said he'd better go home. But he told Jean he'd see her the next day.

" Christmas wouldn't be Christmas, if you didn't drop in," she told him at the door.

When she turned back to Jeff, who was poking at the fire and making sparks fly up the chimney, he said, " Let's go out in the sunroom, shall we? "

She knew what he meant. Betsy had come in to talk to Scotty and was staying around to talk to Jeff. Rick was lying before the fire reading comic books. Mr. Burnaby was sitting where he had sat when Scotty was there, now reading a magazine with great concentration. It seemed as if you could never have a minute alone when you were at home with the Burnabys. It was no wonder Bob and Sally always had some good reason to go out.

But at least there was the sunroom, back of the dining room, where you could talk quietly without having the family enter into the conversation. They found Jimmy curled up on the couch, reading a book about Indians and cowboys.

"Jimmy," said Jean persuasively, "would you mind reading in the living room, where there's a nice fire and everything?"

"I like it here," said Jimmy without raising his head.

"But Jeff and I want to talk," said Jean. "Come on, honey, be nice about things."

She laid her hand on his shoulder and he shrugged it off.

"I'm not going to interrupt you," he protested. "I'm not even going to listen. But this couch is so comfortable I don't feel like going in the other room."

"Honestly!" Jean exploded.

At that moment her mother came in.

"Come on, Jimmy," she said imperatively. "Let Jean and Jeff have this room to themselves."

"Aw!" Reluctantly he got off the couch, his eyes still fixed on his book, and stumbled after his mother into the living room.

"Maybe we should just go out and drive around," Jeff suggested. But Jean shook her head.

"I worked until six," she said, "and all I want to do is sit here with my feet up. Oh, here's your Christmas present, Jeff. Do you want to open it here or at home?"

"Let's open them together," he laid a small white-wrapped box in her lap.

He lifted the heavy square package she had given and said jestingly, "I can tell it isn't Argyle socks, anyway."

"No," she grinned at him. "No Argyles."

He had told her jokingly in the fall that he would be terribly pleased if she would make him some Argyles, as all the other girls were doing for their steady boy friends. She had replied, also jokingly, that she wasn't the knitting type, and he had never mentioned it again. But she knew now that Argyles would have meant far more to him than the book she had chosen.

He laid aside the wrappings and looked at the book.

" Gee, that's swell, Jean. I've been wanting this for a long time. Thanks a lot."

She unwrapped her package, disclosing a small white box from Winter's jewelry store, the most expensive store in Sherwood, where everything from fine glass, china, and silver down to costume jewelry was distinctive. Her heart began to thump a little as she untied the red ribbon. She wished Jeff hadn't spent so much. She wished for a futile moment that she had made him the Argyle socks. Then she opened the box and lifted out a rhinestone necklace.

" O Jeff, how perfectly beautiful! " she cried, sincerely delighted with the pretty thing. " How did you know I needed something like this? "

" Oh, I'm observant," he said. " I saw those green-eyed looks you kept giving all the girls at the formal last fall, I noticed how unadorned you were, and I said to myself, ' Diamonds for my lady for Christmas! ' "

Jean laughed. " The one I got last year broke early in the fall," she said. " I've missed it ever since, and you couldn't have chosen anything I'd like better." She watched the necklace sparkle in the light. " I'll wear it to the Carnival next week. It'll be perfect with that red formal."

" Just what I figured," he said. " Well — I can't wear your book to the Carnival, but I'll sure enjoy it at home."

"Will you be spending Christmas at home this year?"

"Nope, we're going to my cousins' up in Milwaukee. Thank goodness, the roads are clear. We leave about nine. They have a big house, and try to gather in all members of the family within a hundred miles, and Mother felt homesick for Milwaukee this year. I guess we'll come back tomorrow night, but we'll probably be late."

They walked to the front door.

"I'll tell you Merry Christmas now, then," Jean said, matter-of-factly. "If you get home before ten, call me up and I'll say it again."

She stepped outside onto the porch, and he kissed her.

"It's a long day, when I can't call up," he said.

"Oh, we can get together the very next day," she comforted him. "Come on over Saturday afternoon and see our presents."

She walked back to the sunroom when he had gone and looked again at the necklace. It must have cost a lot of money, and she wished he hadn't spent so much. She really would knit him some socks. He had a birthday in April, and she'd try to finish them by that time. That was the least she could do for him, and she wished she felt more enthusiastic about doing it. If she cared for him as as he did for her, she'd enjoy it. But she didn't and couldn't. She put the whole idea of love out of her mind, and went upstairs to collect her presents and put them under the tree.

The younger children had gone to bed. Jean left for church at 10:30. She was singing in the choir for the Christmas Eve service, as she did every year. Sally and Bob were attending the service together. Ricky was serving at the altar.

The tiny St. Paul's Episcopal Church was radiant with candlelight and fragrant with Christmas greens. For Jean, Christmas really began with this service.

Afterward she and Ricky walked home together and Jean thought about the silent, peaceful night.

Christmas.

Each year Christmas seemed like a new starting point in her life, and each year Jean hoped that she could put her mistakes behind her and begin again. Now she thought of Jeff and Kim. Surely this year she could rearrange her life, so that no one would be hurt, so that her friendships would move along without difficulty. Everything was going to be fine from here on, because Christmas was such a good time to start over.

Whispers and scurrying footsteps woke Jean at seven the next morning. Jimmy was standing at the head of the stairs urging his family to hurry up — he couldn't wait another minute. In spite of his urgency, he was reluctant to go down ahead of the others. Half the fun of Christmas is having an audience to witness your excitement, and he wanted all of them to go down and be excited with him.

Betsy hung over the railing analyzing the possibilities in the assorted packages visible from the stairway.

"Mother, aren't you ever going to be ready? What are we waiting for?"

Jean leaped out of bed and threw on her quilted flowered housecoat and slippers and ran a brush through her hair. She followed her family down the steps with the old, familiar enchantment at the sight of the tree piled deep in packages big and small, white tissue, holly-colored wrappings, Christmas bells, red and green, gold and silver ribbons.

Hunting through the packages each member of the family was more interested in finding the presents he was giving to the others than the ones marked for himself.

Jimmy thrust a small package in Jean's lap. "Open it first," he begged. "This is just what you said you wanted."

She shook out of the tissue paper a bright neck scarf and exclaimed, "Why, Jimmy, how did you know I needed a red one?"

"I just remembered you said on Thanksgiving that your red one was worn out," he said, in delight.

Betsy handed her a flat, square present, which turned out to be a piano record of the piece she was studying, and urged her to put it on the machine at once.

It was a wonderful day as always, Jean thought an hour later, helping to collect the scattered wrappings and put them into the fire blazing on the hearth. The Burnabys had more fun giving presents than getting them, but they always loved the ones they got. Jean wished again that she had given Jeff those Argyle socks. She knew now that she would have enjoyed his pleasure in them more than the book she had chosen. Ah, well, she'd get them started this week.

"Somehow I wish I had bought Betsy another doll," said Mrs. Burnaby nostalgically, as they picked up the dishes from the belated breakfast. "I kind of miss dolls at Christmas. Now it's lingerie and records and ice skates. I looked at the dolls last week, and they were beautiful. But Betsy's past them, I'm afraid."

"It does seem funny," Jean agreed, "to have her asking for a tuning fork and a music stand for Christmas presents."

"I hate to let the years go by so fast. I like to hold on

to the things we loved and not forget them."

"Scotty coming in on Christmas was one of the things I always liked," murmured Jean. She wondered if he would come today. He had said he might see them —

At four o'clock he arrived, whistling " Good King Wenceslas " as cheerfully as if he had been waiting for this moment.

"Merry Christmas," said Mrs. Burnaby. "My, it's nice to see you, Scotty. How's your mother now?"

His mother was pretty good, he told her, but she was taking things very easy. She wasn't even sure if she could come over to the Burnabys' Christmas " At Home."

"Dad will come, in any case," he said, " and I'll be back in February to stay. I'm kinda sorry to leave Colorado, but after all, I've had a year and a half out there, and I'd just as soon be at home for a while." He was taking courses that would admit him to law school in his senior year, and the law school at Northern University was very fine.

He looked at everyone's presents, asked Betsy to play him a piece on her new music stand, a suggestion which she accepted very gravely, ignoring the twinkle in his eye. When she did play for him, he told her he was surprised and impressed.

"You go right on with that fiddle," he said. "We could use one around here. Jean sounds kind of lonesome, playing that piano all by herself."

He turned to Jean. "You know it's a kind of tradition with me to hang an ornament on your tree," he reminded her. "I keep asking myself every year how long this is going to go on, and every year I tell myself, 'Well, just this once!' So, here we go again."

He took a small package out of his pocket and handed

112

it to Jean, and she tried to smile as she accepted it. But her heart was beating too fast, and she dropped her eyes to the package in her fingers, hoping they wouldn't shake, hoping that her confusion wouldn't show. Last year it had been a tiny tin angel, with frilled wings. Scotty always thought of the nicest things.

"O Scotty, how darling!"

She lifted from the wrappings a golden Christmas star, which twisted and turned as she held the string, catching and reflecting the lights from the tree.

"How do you find such nice things?" she asked, going over to hang it at the end of a branch, where it turned back and forth in the draft of air through the room.

"It's gotten to be kind of a game with me now," said Scotty, standing beside her. He was close to her shoulder, and she stood very still, touching the star with one finger.

"When I marry a Burnaby girl," he said, jingling the little silver bell he had given Sally two years ago, "I'll expect her to bring all these ornaments as part of her dowry."

Something caught in her throat, and for a minute Jean could not speak. She had felt this way about Scotty last Christmas, but it had worn off, after she had made up her quarrel with Jeff; and when Scotty had come home in the summer he had spent all his time with Ginny Whitaker. Jean had told herself last June that Scotty was just like a big brother. She had faced the fact that he thought she was the "little girl next door" — and here she was all jittery and excited about him again.

She sat down on the couch, impatient with herself, and asked him about his old crowd in Sherwood. Most of the old gang, he told her, were busy with new friends. He'd seen Ted once or twice, but he and Kate were spending most of their time with a couple of friends from Conover who were staying with them for a week. Glen had stayed in California, where he had a dance band and several holiday engagements. Everyone in the old gang seemed to have separated and collected in new groups, and while they had all been getting together and including Scotty in their invitations, still it wasn't the same any more. The only ones he really felt at home with were the Burnabys.

Jean had a feeling that he was lonesome. It was too bad about Ginny Whitaker, she thought. And then she was glad that it was this way.

During the week that followed Christmas, Scotty seemed to drop in almost every day. He liked to talk about Colorado and his friends out there, he was interested in Jean's music, he asked about the high school teachers he had known.

He was so easy to talk to that Jean found herself discussing her own problems. She told him about the grand piano, and he said he'd be holding his thumbs and wishing for it as hard as she was. He was sympathetic about the pressures Betsy's violin put on the family, but he thought Betsy really meant business.

Jean talked about Jeff, hinting at her worry that he was too fond of her. She was too loyal to say outright that she cared less than he did. But between the words she knew that Scotty understood what was troubling her, and sympathized, without offering any suggestions. She told him she was going to knit Jeff some Argyle socks for a surprise and asked Scotty what colors he thought Jeff would like. Then when she had bought the yarn and begun the socks, she wondered, with a rueful smile, if Jeff would appreciate her getting advice about his socks from Scotty.

Several times Jeff had come in while Scotty was there. Always he had been cordial, and they had talked together for a while, until Scotty went home, and Jeff said, more than once, that Scotty was a swell guy — he liked him fine. But toward the end of the week he seemed to be getting restive at finding him at the Burnabys' so often.

"I know he's home for vacation," he grumbled, "and he hasn't got anything to do but be neighborly. But does he have to act like he lived at your house?"

Jean laughed and tried to reassure him.

"He just feels at home with us," she said, and then she warned him, "He's probably going to be around a lot from here on, when he's going to Northern next semester."

Jeff looked as if he didn't like the prospect at all.

Dressing for the Christmas Carnival, four days after Christmas, Jean looked into her eyes in the mirror, wondering why things got out of hand this way. She knew that Jeff was jealous of Scotty, and although she tried to tell herself there was no reason, she could not say it convincingly. In the end she knew it would have been better if she had not tried. The more she explored her own mind and heart in the matter, the more she tried to understand Jeff, the more difficult everything became. The worst of it was that she actually liked him very much, too much to want to hurt him. There was no reason for breaking off with Jeff entirely, and yet the longer they went on, the more he depended on her —

She gave up with a sigh and fastened the rhinestone necklace around her neck, hoping that tonight would be different.

When she walked into the ballroom of the Shoreline

Country Club, which was decorated with artificial snow and icicles, she felt as if she had stepped backward a year. These were all the same girls who had been juniors last year with her. The Nightingales welcomed her pleasantly: most of them had never held it against her that she had resigned from their sorority. Barbara Keller had come again with Mark Hamilton who had won the high senior award last year. This year he was going to Princeton, and Barbara told the girls in the dressing room that he had written before Thanksgiving to say that he wanted to take her to the Carnival during the holidays when he came home. Last year Barbara and Mark had looked devoted. This year they looked like old friends reminiscing over other days.

Jean and Jeff moved onto the floor, and she remembered that Tom last year had not been an interesting dancer. Jeff was much, much better, and for an hour she thought how well they matched each other's steps. They stood by the windows overlooking the frozen lake, watching the surf toss up from under masses of ice, and Jeff appreciated it as Jean did. He had his arm about her as they looked out, and she knew that looking at the lake this year meant more to him than it did to her.

It was a better party than last year, she thought, better than some of their dates with Kim and Tony. Only this time, when she was with Jeff alone, she seemed to feel the weight of his feeling; she had now to watch her words, to be sure she didn't say anything he might take amiss, or reveal anything she hadn't planned for him to know. Jeff never used to be like this, she thought sadly. Why did love have to be this way? If he could just keep it light —

116

On the way home she was very quiet, trying to figure out how to handle the situation so that no one would be hurt. Perhaps she could hold the *status quo* until just next summer, when they would separate for vacation, and then they would go away to college next year and everything would take care of itself.

"I never hoped to be able to go away to school," she said conversationally, "knowing how hard everything will be for the folks by the time two of us are in school. But Miss Austin says there's a good chance of my getting this scholarship for Overton — wouldn't it be wonderful?"

"You'll get it," he said, with heart-warming confidence in his girl's being able to do anything. "Overton, huh? Say I've heard that's a darn good place. Small school, but good. Why don't I plan to go to the same place? We could have a wonderful time."

"We certainly could," Jean said automatically, feeling trapped. "But Overton might not be strong in science, and I thought science was what you wanted. I shouldn't think you'd choose your college because of your girl friend!" She laughed, trying to keep it humorous. But Jeff was serious.

"I think Overton could give me what I want in undergrad work," he said. "It's the graduate school that makes the difference. This is really an idea! Couldn't we have fun together?"

He was looking at the snowy road ahead, his lips curved in anticipation, his eyes sparkling. Jean looked at him for a moment and felt a pang of pity.

What could she say?

"Loads of fun," she assented, hoping her voice was properly enthusiastic.

CHAPTER 10

BY the time Kim returned from Mexico Jean found herself looking forward with keen anticipation to seeing her again. The best thing about Kim, Jean felt, was her independence. She was companionable and stimulating, without being demanding. They had a wonderful time when they were together, but the plans were not irrevocable. If Jean had to cancel a trip to Chicago, or tell Kim she was going to be too busy to see her Friday after school, she never had to make explanations, or worry about what Kim was going to think. With Jeff there were hurt feelings or disappointed hopes, or even, Jean always suspected, a lurking idea that she didn't really want to be with him, and the need for always allaying those reactions was becoming oppresive. With Kim she felt like a free agent, with no emotional strings attached.

Kim invited her to the first Saturday matinee of *Seventeen,* the week before it opened in Chicago the middle of January.

"I got a couple of tickets the moment they were put on sale," she said. "You know, I told you about this show. Nicky Trumbull, the boy I went with in New York last summer, is in it, and we've been writing ever since I left New York. He told me he'd see me when the show came to Chicago. I'll introduce you to him. He's simply wonderful. Some day he's going to be a star."

The idea of meeting a member of the cast of a New York show sounded even more thrilling than seeing the show itself, and Jean was deeply excited about it, although she said nothing to her mother about the plans to go backstage. Mrs. Burnaby was less than enthusiastic about the invitation.

"I suppose it's all right, as long as it's just a matinee," she said pessimistically. "I never feel quite sure about Kim."

"But, Mother," Jean protested, "we're almost eighteen years old — what could possibly happen? We're just going to a matinee in Chicago!"

"I know," her mother conceded. "There isn't any real reason why you shouldn't go — but I wish there were."

Kim drove down in the blue Victoria.

"Mother thinks I've got holes in my head to insist on driving to Chicago," Kim said with a grin. "She says the parking is so bad. But I say the trains are even worse, and when Daddy said there was a good garage near the theater, she didn't object too much."

Jean was not worried about parking. It was delightful to drive down along the Outer Drive, instead of riding the rattly, drafty, noisy interurban. The day was cold and overcast. Over the lake the clouds looked threatening, and Jean loved it. They were thirty minutes early, and Kim parked the car in the garage her father had recommended, two blocks from the theater, with no difficulty whatever.

They settled themselves in the front row balcony seats

twenty minutes before curtain time, and read through the programs. Kim had bought a large, illustrated pamphlet about the cast.

"This is Nicky," she pointed to a picture on one of the last pages. "He hasn't got much of a part in this, but the critics in New York just raved about the way he handled it."

"How did you meet him?" Jean was deeply interested in this professional friend of Kim's.

"Oh, a friend of Dad's had a big theater party last June," Kim said, as if she loved to recall it. "There were crowds of people there, and Nicky was one of them. It was so romantic. We were both standing by the supper table filling plates, and he looked straight at me and said: 'I've been waiting for you. What took you so long?' So I laughed and said: 'I've hunted and hunted, and couldn't find you. And here you are and I don't even know your name.' Then he laughed and we introduced ourselves, and after that we were together all evening. He sent me flowers the next day, and we went out several times."

She stared at the curtain, lost in thought, and Jean thought it was the most romantic thing she'd ever heard.

"Dad doesn't like him," Kim said abruptly. "You know, it's funny about fathers. He doesn't pay any attention to what I do, and he never worries. Most of the time he treats me just like a grownup. And then, just when you don't expect it, he gets upset about something. Like Nicky. There were lots of other men and boys I dated at different times that he might have worried about if he'd known them. But no! He always thought I could take care of myself. And then when Nicky comes along – the only one who really matters – he says: 'I don't like that fellow,

120

Kim. Don't have anything to do with him.' But he wouldn't give me any reasons."

"Sometimes parents are like that," Jean agreed, thinking of her own.

"It didn't really matter," said Kim. "I just never mentioned Nicky again, and Dad forgot about him. But I did keep on seeing him, and he's been writing since we left New York. He's going to be very successful, you can just tell. So much personality! The stage is the only thing he really cares about —"

The house darkened; the curtain was going up. Jean watched the play with an interest she had never felt before. Nicky had a very small part, but Jean was inclined to agree with Kim that he was outstanding. She could not have said whether or not she would have noticed him without Kim's special interest to call him to her attention.

She forgot herself completely in the play. When it was over, she hated to return to the world again. She felt, with Kim, that the theater held glamour and excitement and dreams come true, and she could understand Kim's yearning to be part of it.

The curtain went down finally after innumerable curtain calls. Nicky took a bow with the cast at the end.

"Hurry," said Kim. "I told him I'd see him right after the show. There's a special exit near the stage door."

Still dreaming about the play, Jean collected her wraps and gloves and followed Kim, feeling as if she were about to enter the dream world she had been watching on the stage.

As they made their way through the audience crowding to the exits and stood in line, hearing comments on the play, the weather, and the hour of the day, the spell began to evaporate. Jean looked at her watch. Five twenty.

"It's getting awfully late," she said to Kim. "Are you sure you can find him quickly?"

"Oh, sure!" said Kim. "I wrote him I'd be there, and he'll be looking for us. Why? Is your mother expecting you early?"

"I told her I thought we'd be back by 6:30," said Jean. "Look — he's your friend, after all. He won't care about meeting me. Maybe I should go on over and take the train home, and then you won't have to hurry at all."

"Oh, no!" protested Kim. "Here we are, right now, at the door. By the time you walk three blocks to the train and wait fifteen or twenty minutes, you won't get home any sooner than if you wait for me. Really — I'm not going to talk to Nicky for more than five minutes. We'll be on our way in twenty minutes, and you wouldn't be on a train by that time."

Jean allowed herself to be persuaded. Kim's argument was reasonable. The trains were slow, with frequent stops and long delays in changing trains, to reach Sherwood. More than likely she would get home sooner by going with Kim.

They reached the stage door and waited. Kim said Nicky would be watching for her. The cast emerged, one by one, to greet waiting friends and find a place for a quick supper before returning for the evening perform-ance. Some teen-agers were chattering and giggling rau-cously, teasing each other about autographs and crushes, and Jean looked at them with distaste. She hoped that she and Kim would not be associated with such rowdy be-havior. Glancing at Kim, she was sure that they looked adult and dignified, compared with the conspicuous bob-by-soxers clamoring around them.

She was beginning to worry about the time. It was five thirty now, and they should be on their way inside of ten minutes if they were to be home on time. A few flakes of snow were drifting down from the darkened sky, and Jean's feet were cold. She wondered if she should declare positively that she was going home on the train. The anticipation of meeting Nicky Trumbull had worn off, anyway. But at that moment they moved inside the door, where it was warm again, although dingy and unswept.

Kim looked along the closed doors before them.

" I don't know which would be his dressing room," she said. " The star is over there. Some day Nick's door will have a star on it. I suppose he's in with someone else. Oh, well, he'll come out in a minute! "

Jean tried to command herself to patience. But as the minutes crawled by, and the cluster of people around them thinned out, she became more and more restive. She should have taken the train half an hour ago, she told herself futilely. She should have known something like this would happen. Now it was so late that she really would get home sooner with Kim.

" Nicky! " Kim cried in a gay, sophisticated voice that Jean had not heard her use before. Jean looked up quickly. Kim was holding out both hands to a dark, handsome youth with a sullen expression. His face changed as he saw her, and he grasped both her hands.

" Kim! How nice to see you! I had no idea you'd be here."

Kim had said he was expecting her, Jean remembered, but no matter.

" Jean, I want you to meet my friend, Nicky Trumbull,"

123

Kim pulled Jean forward. Nicky acknowledged the introduction indifferently, and Kim chattered on. "How is New York? And how do you like Chicago? We love it here. I'm crushed that we're only to be here a year. The play was simply terrific, Nicky. I thought you were most outstanding."

He looked alive and intense. "Did you really, Kim? You don't know how it does me good to hear you say that. Nobody knows how it's going to catch on here. One critic liked it, one was neutral. We'd like it to run till June, of course."

He seemed to care about nothing but the show.

Kim said, "Can we get together sometime while you're here?"

Jean admired the way she kept her voice casual, the way she accepted his verdict without betraying disappointment when he said, with only a trace of regret: "I don't know, honey. I've been hoping. But we're on a terrific schedule of rehearsals and performances, and I've got to stay close to the shop. What's your number? Maybe we can talk on the telephone."

He wrote it on the back of a crumpled visiting card he pulled out of his pocket, and Kim said nonchalantly: "You must get out for supper, Nicky, and Jean and I've got to get back to Sherwood. It's wonderful knowing you're in town. Good luck!"

Her timing was perfect. Nicky would have excused himself in another thirty seconds, and Kim was quick enough to do it first.

He smiled at her then, and for a few seconds his personality was warm and sunny, and Jean could see, as through a veil, something of his appeal for Kim.

"Thanks so much for coming around, Kim. You do me lots of good — you know that, don't you? I'll be talking to you."

With a quick wave of her hand, Kim left him. It was a good exit, Jean thought, following her through the alley to the sidewalk, where the theater entrance stood empty and littered with discarded programs. Kim was independent with Nicky too, and that was a good way to be. Jean wondered exactly how much there was in the affair Kim had described to her. How much did Kim really care? And did Nicky care at all? Perhaps they were both concealing their feelings because she was there.

Then Jean put behind her all thought of the show and Nicky, and concentrated on getting home. It was 6:15 now, and she was going to be late again. She wondered if she should telephone her family. But she shouldn't be more than half an hour late now, and she dreaded telling them over the telephone that Kim had gotten her into a spot like this again, and how could she tell them the reason? She thought of what her father would say about hanging around a stage door for forty minutes, and she decided that she would have to tell him face to face, if it must come out. To tell him over the telephone and then be late arriving after he had been brooding over it in her absence would be intolerable.

At the garage, there was a ten minute wait for the car. Jean and Kim sat on a bench inside the door and watched the light, steady snowfall. The streets were white now, and it seemed to be getting heavier. But at long last they were in the car and crawling across the Loop, delayed at every block by traffic lights and early evening traffic. When they turned into the Outer Drive, it was 6:40, and

Kim became suddenly aware of the time.

"I didn't realize it was getting so late," she said, stepping on the accelerator. "Of course there wasn't a thing we could do about it. I get so frustrated when things combine like this to make me late. Maybe I'm jinxed that way. We can make time on the Drive, though."

She talked about Nicky then, developing the whole story, and taking Jean into her confidence in a way she never had before.

"Don't let anyone know I've seen him," she cautioned Jean, slowing down as she took a turn. "Dad is so unreasonable about it that it's just better if he doesn't know. If he finds out that I've seen him, and I'm going to see him again, I'm just going to run away and marry him. Nicky asked me in New York, and I thought it would be better to wait and finish high school. But if Dad is going to interfere, I'm not even going to finish. Nicky is too important — "

She concentrated on her driving, her mouth drawn into a determined line, and Jean watched the snow whirling into the headlights, feeling as if she ought to be surprised at Kim's revelation, and yet somehow not surprised. Remembering Nicky's manner, she thought he could be the type who was desperately in love with Kim, and frustrated because they were kept apart. Something told her that he might just as easily not be in love with Kim at all. But surely Kim was too smart and too sophisticated to have dreamed up the whole situation?

No, Jean was convinced that Kim was perfectly capable not only of running away to marry Nicky, but of persuading him to go through with it as well. She remembered Mrs. Ballard's words last Thanksgiving: "You may not know how much we count on you, Jean," and then, " Take care of my little girl."

She had no business delegating her responsibility, Jean thought, half rejecting the assignment. But if she could prevent Kim from doing anything foolish, perhaps she could influence the girl where her parents could not.

Her thoughts were tossed apart suddenly, as, without warning, the car slid smoothly sideways, and Jean heard a crunch of metal, a crumpling, tearing, menacing sound. They stopped with a jolt, as if they had hit a curb. Jean stared at Kim, whose face was set and pale.

" We hit something," Kim muttered. " How bad? "

Jean looked out of the window beside her. A black sedan was wedged between their back wheels and the curb of the Drive. A man in a gray coat and soft hat, with a maroon muffler, was looking at the front fender of his car. He turned toward Kim's car, and Jean lowered her window, which worked badly.

" Was anyone hurt? " Jean asked.

" Nobody hurt," he said grimly. " But my car is sure knocked out of commission."

Kim and Jean looked at each other, and Kim leaned over to the open window.

" I'm terribly sorry," she said. " I don't even know what happened."

" You skidded on the snow," he said. " You were driving too fast, young lady. Anybody that knows how to drive would know you can't drive that speed on this kind of snow. Pavements greasy and slick. You just slid into me — and it's a lucky thing we didn't mess up a lot more cars."

Jean tried to open her door, but it seemed to be jammed. Both girls got out on the driver's side, and walked around to look at the damage. The front fender and bumper of the black car were tangled with the back fender and bumper of Kim's car.

"I tried to slow down and get out of your way," the other driver said. "I wasn't too keen about being around you at your speed, and you were passing me. But I couldn't even slow down on this stuff very quickly — and then, wham, you got me!"

"What do we do next?" Kim asked plaintively. "I'm insured —"

"Gimme the name of your company," the man said, getting out a notebook and pencil. Kim found her identification card and gave him the information he wanted. A police car stopped in front of them, a red light blinking ominously as the policeman came toward them. Jean's knees were shaking, although her mind felt clear. She wondered how soon they could go on — whether, indeed, they could go on at all — and how they were going to get home.

Kim answered questions, produced licenses, gave her version of what had happened. Jean told what she knew. The other driver told his story. The girls climbed back into the car and waited.

"How long do we have to wait?" Jean wondered. "Can't we just go on?"

The policeman told them, when he was asked, that he doubted if the cars could be disentangled until a garageman came along. He expressed the opinion that both cars would run, but it would take more manpower than he could offer to pry them apart.

They waited an hour. An hour and ten minutes. An hour and twenty minutes.

"What on earth is keeping them?" Jean muttered. She got out of the car again and went to ask the policeman how long it would be.

"This kind of weather every emergency service is busy, Miss," he told her. "You'll be lucky to get out of here in a couple of hours."

Jean sat in the car and stared out of the window resentfully. None of this had really been Kim's fault, she thought. Not the snow, nor the skidding, although perhaps she had been driving too fast for the road condition. Not the delay at the garage, nor the delay now, waiting for help. Only, she couldn't help thinking, if they had started home on time before the rush set in, before they would have felt they had to hurry, none of this would have happened — probably. She couldn't face what her parents would be thinking by now. And there was no way to telephone from the edge of the Outer Drive.

The garageman arrived at last with the tow truck. The cars were separated, Kim's car, with a battered fender and a jammed right-hand door, would run, and the policeman, somewhat sympathetically, told them to get along home and not to have any more trouble. Kim drove slowly and carefully into Sherwood at 9:30.

"This is a mess," Kim said regretfully, "and I'm terribly sorry, Jean. I guess it was just one of those things no one could help. Just don't say anything about Nicky, remember. And after all, he had nothing to do with the accident."

Her father and mother looked drawn and tense as Jean faced them at 9:35.

"Well, what is it this time?" her father demanded. "I suppose Kim had to chase another fire engine?"

"Nothing like that." Jean discovered that she was exhausted clear through. She hung up her coat, brushing off the snow with limp motions, and sagged down on the couch.

"We were just coming along the Outer Drive, and the car skidded sideways on the snow and rammed another car into the curb. Nobody was hurt," she said hastily, at the expression on their faces. "And I couldn't telephone. We had to wait for a garageman to pry the cars apart, and all the emergency men were busy tonight, so we had to wait a long time."

She closed her eyes, wishing she didn't have to talk about it any more. She was tired of the whole thing, bone-tired.

"What time was all this going on?" her father demanded.

"Oh —" she had looked at her watch, Jean remembered, just as they crunched, "seven o'clock!"

"And how far down the Drive?"

"Montrose, the policeman said."

"What I don't see is why you were only coming past Montrose at seven," he said very sternly. "If you'd come home right after the matinee, you'd have been here by 6:30. What were you doing in the meantime?"

Thinking fast, Jean said, "We got delayed leaving the theater, there was such a crowd. And then we had to wait at the garage for the car —"

"I never heard of being delayed over an hour in getting away from a theater," said her mother. She sounded as if she were not so much criticizing Jean as trying to straighten out in her own mind all the pieces of an intricate puzzle. Defensively Jean thought, She would criti-

130

cize fast enough if I told her everything. She dared not mention Nicky. Kim trusted her to keep that a secret. Wearily Jean closed her eyes.

"What were you doing around the theater until after 6:30?" Mr. Burnaby asked. He sounded as if he intended to get to the bottom of things. Jean threw out her hands in desperation.

"We weren't there until 6:30," she protested. "We got away as soon as we could. Kim saw a — a friend, and we stopped to talk for a minute, and we couldn't seem to break it off right away — "

Her mother and father exchanged looks that said, There is more to this than Jean is telling.

"I wish you'd let me alone," Jean cried passionately, close to tears. She got up from the couch and started for the stairs.

"All right, honey," said her mother, unexpectedly surrendering, with a sidewise glance at Jean's father. "Only I wish you'd not plan to go places with Kim any more. I don't know why these things always seem to happen with her!"

Jean's protest died in her throat. Her mother was right. And Jean didn't even want to go anywhere with Kim again. But of course she couldn't say that. She looked at the clock.

"You'd better call Jeff," her mother said, seeing her glance. "He was here at eight for a date. He waited till quarter past nine, and he seemed worried when he left."

"I'll call from upstairs," said Jean.

She knew that her parents were worried about more than the accident, and she wished she could explain things. Jeff asked the same questions her father had asked, but with him she could be more outspoken.

"We just got delayed starting home," Jean said, not concealing the impatience in her tone. "No, I can't say anything more about it. The accident held us up a couple of hours after we did start. Jeff, you know I meant to be here, and I'm sorry I missed our date, but there wasn't a thing I could do about it."

Hanging up the telephone after a conversation that went on much too long, she had a sickening conviction that no one believed her. They weren't blaming her, exactly, but Jeff and her parents both felt she was concealing something. And so she was, she admitted to herself, but there was no choice.

She felt as if she were caught in a net, and what could she do about it?

CHAPTER 11

IF her parents and Jeff had let the subject of Kim alone, Jean felt, everything would have been simpler. She had resolved not to see so much of Kim for the rest of the year, telling herself that they weren't good for each other. She reasoned that perhaps Kim was not so irresponsible when she was alone, although she acknowledged that she knew nothing about Kim's affairs when she was not with her. Kim didn't mention Nicky in school, and when Jean thought of it, she realized that Kim didn't talk about herself very much anyway.

But Jeff could not let the subject drop. On their next date he kept asking about what had happened and making uncomplimentary remarks about Kim until Jean grew impatient.

"Forget it," she said sharply. "I know you don't like her — you don't have to keep harping on it. I'm tired of hearing about Kim."

But Jeff's insistence, coupled with her parents' queries about what Kim was doing these days and their checking up on Jean's whereabouts from day to day, aroused in her a defensive reaction that counteracted her own resolutions not to see so much of Kim. Jean began to feel that no one understood Kim. Kim's mother was counting on Jean to be a friend to her daughter. Besides, Kim was fun. As the days slipped past and the accident on the Outer Drive as well as the meeting with Nicky Trumbull became obscured by the quickening pace at the high school, as the orchestra began planning its spring concert and the spring play went into rehearsal, caution seemed needless, and Kim's company harmless.

The annual Gilbert and Sullivan production was scheduled for the last week in March, and Jean was singing, as in former years, in the chorus. Kim was one of the leads. Her voice was outstanding among high school singers, and she showed a fine sense of comedy in the part. As the rehearsals progressed, even Jeff's annoyance with Kim faded out. She was so amusing during rehearsal, she showed a dependable feeling for co-operation with both cast and director, and she offered some excellent suggestions for other parts in such a friendly manner that both cast and director felt she was contributing a great deal to the production.

Rehearsals took most afternoons after school, and Kim was busy three Saturdays in a row, while Jean was making up practicing time. Jean began to feel a pleasant conviction that everything was straightening itself out, just as she had known it would.

The first week of February, Scotty came home to go to school at Northern University. There was no fanfare about his arrival this time. He had been home two days before Jean saw him going into his door late one afternoon. He waved to her and called, " I'll be over one of these days."

She had been looking forward to his coming back to

Sherwood to stay, and now that she knew he was back, she felt as if the thing she had been waiting for was accomplished and the suspense was ended.

She went on inside to find Betsy practicing her violin. Betsy had worked up to second violin in the elementary orchestra, after having started in sixth place, and she was a little smug about her progress. After twenty minutes she put her instrument away.

" How long did you practice? " Jean asked.

" Long enough," pronounced Betsy, " I've done all my pieces."

" How about your exercises? "

" They're all right," Betsy sounded annoyed. " I hate exercises. Anyway, my teacher says I'm doing just fine."

" Scotty is home," Jean said. " He'll want to hear you one of these days."

" I'm not doing any more exercises today, no matter who's home," announced Betsy. " Scales! I'd like to see you play a scale on the violin! "

Mrs. Burnaby came in from the kitchen looking determined.

" Betsy, after all we've gone through to let you have that violin, the least you can do is practice the way your teacher asks you to."

Incensed, Betsy snatched her violin out of the case again.

" Sometimes I feel like smashing the old thing," she muttered.

Jean and her mother looked at each other, as Betsy sawed exasperatedly through a scale.

" I haven't got as much faith in talent as I had," Mrs. Burnaby murmured. " But her teacher insists it's just temperament, and she'll get over it. She says nobody likes to practice."

Jean shrugged. "I didn't until a couple of years ago. I guess it's just one more problem for you."

"How anybody raises a musician I don't know," Mrs. Burnaby sighed. "Our life seems very complicated since we took a violin into the family."

But as Betsy worked under duress her annoyance faded, her round face took on a look of concentration, and she repeated one passage six times.

"Jean, will you play the piano with me for this piece?" she asked, at last.

Jean sat down, and a deep satisfaction filled her. It was strange and wonderful how all her problems faded when she was playing the piano, especially with a violin. She hadn't played with Kim for several weeks, and suddenly she wanted to again. When Betsy was finished, Jean went to the telephone and called Kim.

"Let's get together on Saturday and have some music," she said.

"Good," said Kim promptly. "I was just thinking today that it's been a long time. How about that sonata for violin and piano?"

Hanging up the telephone Jean thought, That's what is really wonderful about Kim. Regardless of what her parents thought and worried over, Kim was a very satisfactory companion. Jean had never known anyone else with whom she could play the piano with such pleasure.

The Saturday afternoon session was as good as she had known it would be. Neither of the girls cared about having an audience, and both played for their own pleasure. But Betsy sat around and drank it in, saying only, "Someday I'll play like that." And Scotty came over around four, for the first time since he'd been home, and stayed until six, impressed not only with Kim's fiddle but with Jean's piano. He was interested to hear about the Gilbert and Sullivan production, in which he had sung one of the leads himself two years before, and Jean promised to get him tickets for the first performance, since the last two were already sold out.

The week before the final performance on Saturday night, Kim organized a cast party. Cast parties were nothing new, since they followed almost every dramatic production. But everyone felt this one was going to be superlative. Kim told Jean that fifteen of the principals and chorus were going to start out at Tony's house with Cokes and food, and move on every couple of hours to another house, until they wound up somewhere for breakfast.

" We're not sure yet where the breakfast is going to be," Kim said, her eyes sparkling. " I said, wouldn't it be terrific to have a bonfire on the beach at five o'clock in the morning, and watch the sun rise as we cook bacon over the fire — all wrapped in blankets, of course."

They both giggled at the idea of a beach picnic in March at five o'clock in the morning. But the party was discussed all week, and everyone felt sure that it was going to be filled with the most ingenious and unusual activities that could be devised. From day to day some new stunt was suggested and added to the program. Even Jeff thought the party sounded terrific.

" Now about tonight," Jean prepared her parents on Saturday afternoon. " This is the final performance, and we're having this cast party afterward that I've been telling you about. So don't worry if I don't get home till about nine o'clock in the morning."

She said it with casual assurance, hoping that her very confidence would hoodwink her parents into accepting the party without any further questions.

"What do you mean, in the morning?" her father demanded. "When did this all-night idea get around?"

"Daddy, they always have an all-night party after a big performance," said Jean very patiently. "It's like Senior Prom or something — it's just *the* thing to do."

"Not around here it isn't," he said, just as casually as she had made her announcement. "It's taken me quite a lot of effort to go along with this all-night nonsense for Senior Prom. But that's the only time. Now, don't argue about it, Jean," he warned, as she prepared to make a rebellious protest. "As long as Jeff is going with you, you can celebrate this big occasion until two o'clock. And as far as I'm concerned, even two o'clock is stretching things quite a bit. But that's the deadline. And if you don't want to go on that basis, you don't need to go at all."

Jean closed her mouth and looked at her mother piteously.

"I'm sorry, honey," said Mrs. Burnaby. "But your father is absolutely right. There is no reason for high school students to stay out all night just for fun any time there seems to be something to celebrate, and this is no exception."

Jean knew there was nothing more to be said and although she seethed and rebelled inside, to Kim and the rest of the gang, that night, she upheld her parents gallantly.

"My folks said two o'clock is my limit," she reported brightly, during make-up. "But don't mind me — I don't really care. We'll have a wonderful time anyway."

At least by being loyal to her parents she had saved herself from their sympathy. The rest of the group made no criticism, either of her parents or of her own position, the general attitude being the same as if she had announced a conflict in equally desirable dates: they were sorry she couldn't stay out with them, but they couldn't blame her.

They left the high school after the final, successful performance in three cars, Jean and Jeff riding in Kim's car, with Tony at the wheel. At Tony's house they found Cokes and potato chips in the recreation room, and Jean played the old upright piano for them, while they sang over again all the songs from the show. It was more delightful singing parts and choruses in a small group than it had been even in rehearsal and performance, and Kim and Tony did a duet together, " None Shall Part Us," that was encored twice.

" I never enjoyed a play so much," Jean said to Jeff, as they sang again the rousing chorus. When they had exhausted the repertoire of *Iolanthe,* they began to recall songs from earlier productions, in which most of them had taken part.

At one o'clock someone said: " Hey, I'm hungry. Anyone else want a hamburger? "

" Let's go out to Andy's," cried Kim. " He's open all night, and his hamburgers are divine."

Andy was a large, genial host, who enjoyed the high school clientele, and who ran the kind of restaurant where parents did not mind their sons and daughters going. And he really did make the best hamburgers in town. The party piled into the three cars again, and Dave Singer squabbled with Tony about driving the blue Victoria, which was the only new model among the three cars.

"My, how nice to be popular!" sighed Kim, getting out of the way. "Maybe you'd just like to take the car out and leave me at home?"

The girls giggled, the boys guffawed, and Tony pushed Dave out on the sidewalk and got behind the wheel. At Andy's they discovered another cast party and exchanged hilarious comments on the occasion.

It seemed as if the evening was only beginning when Jean looked at her watch and discovered that it was five minutes of two. The most perfect evening she had ever spent was being cut short, and she thought she couldn't stand it. Even Jeff had been lighthearted and gay tonight, laughing at Kim as if he liked her. Jean couldn't bear to leave the party.

"Kids," she said, "let's stop a minute at my house and I'll tell the folks that everything is O.K. and I'm going on. If I don't let them know, they'll worry."

The three cars lined up before the Burnaby house and one of them sounded a raucous horn. Jeff got out of the car with Jean.

"Hey, you guys," he said, going back to the noisy car, "use your heads. People on this street are all asleep. If you wake them up, Jean's dad will probably be so mad he won't let her stay out."

Obligingly every car became quiet, save for submerged scuffles and giggles in back seats, as Jeff went up to the door with Jean.

Opening it gently, she whispered, "You wait here and I'll see if they're awake."

But before she had finished, her mother called: "Is that you, Jean? Be sure to lock the door before you come up."

"I'm not coming up just yet, Mother," said Jean. "The party is just getting going, and I wanted to let you know I'm going on with them."

There was a long silence, as her mother hesitated a moment, went back to her room, and returned to the stairs with Jean's father.

"You wait outside for me, Jeff. I'll be right out," Jean whispered. Her father and mother came down in bathrobes.

To her parents she said: "O Mother, this is the most wonderful evening! We've been singing all the operettas over again, and we just got hamburgers at Andy's. The gang is going on now to Dave's house, and then we're all winding up at Tony's house for breakfast."

Her mother looked at her father. Mr. Burnaby said: "No, you're not, Jean. It's been a good party, and now it's over. Did Jeff come up with you to the door?"

"He's waiting for me on the porch." Her heart began to beat with a frantic tripping sensation, and she was in a desperate hurry to finish this discussion and get away from uncertainty. "All the kids are waiting outside. Dad, this time I'm staying with them. I don't care about Senior Prom, I don't care about anything. This is the party I want to stay out for, and they're all expecting me."

"You're not going on," said her father. "It's after two o'clock, and for you the party is over. We're glad you had a good time, but we can't see any reason to prolong things forever. You know the rule."

"Dad, I've *got* to go with them," Jean protested. To her horror her eyes were filling with tears, and her voice was shaking.

Her father shook his head.

141

"You've got to stay home," he said positively. "Now, do you want to go out and tell them good night, or shall I?"

It was a hideous alternative. Jean could not see how she could bear to tell all those friends that she had to go to bed at two o'clock like a baby. But it was even worse to think of her father telling them for her. She shook her head hopelessly.

"I can't tell them."

Her father opened the door.

"Don't you go," she cried hastily. "Let Jeff do it."

She never knew how she pulled herself together in that moment of tragedy. But as Jeff came to the door she managed a bright smile, and her voice shook only a little.

"Jeff, Dad says no. Will you tell the kids I can't go with them?"

His expression of sympathy almost broke her down. For one distraught moment she wanted to weep on his shoulder.

"Sure thing, Mr. Burnaby," Jeff said. "Maybe you're right, at that. I don't think I'm staying out much longer. See you tomorrow, Jean."

He went back to the waiting cars with a trotting step, and Jean closed the door, not wanting to hear what he said, nor see the faces staring at her in unbearable pity.

"You've ruined my whole senior year," she stormed at her father. "This was the best party I've ever been on, in my whole high school career, and you've spoiled it all."

Her mother started to speak, but Jean rushed past her and up the stairs to the seclusion of her own room. She was the only girl in the whole school who had parents like hers, taking all the joy out of life, interfering with her plans, keeping her away from her friends. She wondered

142

hopelessly why her parents couldn't be like the Ballards, who were so easy to live with. They understood what Kim needed — freedom and independence, and being allowed to grow up. She cried herself to sleep.

In the morning she was heavy-eyed and grieved, remembering the moment she opened her eyes the blight that had settled over her life. She soaked her face in cold water, trying to think of some way to make her parents sorry for this unbearable restriction. The cold water woke her up, and although she was still deeply angered at her parents, she did not feel quite so bitter as she had last night. Wrapped in chilly hauteur, and determined to speak to no one unnecessarily, she descended the stairs on Sunday morning, hoping her father would realize someday what he had done to her.

A piece of brown paper covered the floor at the foot of the stairs by the front door. She looked down at a great black X, as it crackled under her foot, and read the inscription in heavy crayon:

"X marks the spot where the world came to an end last night."

Involuntarily her lips twitched, and then she began to laugh. Trust Dad to figure out something like this! She told herself she was still angry, but as she looked at the X, she could feel her anger fading.

Her father looked up from the Sunday paper, as she came into the dining room, and regarded her solemnly.

"Can you eat, honey?"

"I guess so," Jean admitted.

He came over and put his arm around her shoulders.

"I know you have the meanest parents in the whole town," he confessed. "But we just can't help it. I guess we're made this way. Try and live with it."

Again her lips twitched. "I'm getting used to it," she said.

"Someday you'll treat your own children the same way," he told her.

Jean was about to argue. She wanted to say, "I'll let them stay out all night every week if they want to," and then she knew she wouldn't.

"I suppose I will," she agreed. "Might as well take it out on someone." They smiled at each other then, and Jean surrendered her last resentment. Oh, well, she thought, it's just as comfortable not to stay mad — especially when you can't win.

That last Sunday in March was warm and balmy. When Jean came home from church, the bright sun and soft air revived her spirits until she wanted to skip and dance for spring. In the front lawn early crocuses were budding, and the first tiny tulip spears showed through the unkempt ground.

"I feel just like working in the garden," said her mother at the dinner table. "It will probably snow tomorrow, but today is spring, and I'm going to rake out the old leaves and see what's coming up."

Jean joined her, not because she loved gardening, but because the new season called her out of doors. Next door Scotty was raking his yard.

"If this keeps up, we can play badminton any week end," he said across the fence. "Come on over and see what's happening in our garden."

Jean stood her rake against a tree and went over to the Scotts' yard, to look at their daffodils, tulips, crocuses, all of them faint green promises.

They sat down on a bench he had hauled out of the garage, and began to talk. Scotty asked about Kim, and that led to the cast party and Jean told him of her bitter frustration.

"You're doing all right," he told her. "When I was in school I used to hear about those all-night parties. They got kind of rough, most of the time, and lots of the girls' parents wouldn't let them stay out after one or two."

Jean stared at the barren treetops. "I think the leaves are beginning to bud out," she said with a quick excitement. "Look — can't you see little roughnesses on the branches up there?"

Scotty stared at the trees and nodded. "Spring will come," he said with conviction.

Jean laughed. "I think you're a lot like my father," she said, unaware of the pride that crept into her voice. "He always knows about things."

"Men do," Scotty told her. "I know how you felt about the party — as if you'd missed half your life in one night. But I'll bet you dollars to dimes, right this minute, that you'll find the rest of the night wasn't as much fun as the part you were there for."

She looked at him doubtfully, "You think not?"

"I know it," he said emphatically.

"So Dad was only trying to save me from bitter disappointment," she said ironically.

"Why, sure," said Scotty, laughing.

"I'll tell you the rest of the story when I hear it," she promised.

She could hardly wait to ask Kim on Monday morning about the end of the party.

"What happened after I left you kids on Saturday

night? " Jean asked, the minute she met Kim at the lockers. Kim hung up her windbreaker, and combed out her hair before the mirror on the door.

"It was simply sensational," she said, smiling at Jean through the mirror, with her dimple deeper than ever. That should show Scotty, Jean thought. Kim went on, "We went over to Dave's house after you left, and Mimi went to sleep on the couch. So the rest of us sat around and talked — you know."

Jean knew.

"And then we played canasta for a couple of hours, until Mimi woke up. And then it slowed down — nobody wanted to sing any more, or dance. Joann and Dick got pinned — but I don't think it counts. I think it was just something to pass the time myself. So then at six o'clock we all went down to the lake front to see the sun rise. One of the boys fell in the lake and got soaked, and Dick and Joann took him home. Tony ran my car into the sand, and we couldn't get out — everybody pushed and pushed, but we were stuck till eight o'clock. It was simply freezing, before the sun came up, and we were all starving. But we finally got out, after Tony found a couple of pieces of plank to run under the wheels. I was dead yesterday — everyone was dead. But we had a marvelous time."

It was surprising, Jean thought, that it didn't sound marvelous. In fact, it sounded a little dull, and she knew that she would have been bored long before they got stuck in the sand. She still wished she had been able to stay with them, but she had to acknowledge that she hadn't missed as much as she had thought Saturday night.

"What did your folks say when you came in?" she asked, touching up her lips.

146

Kim shrugged. "Oh, they didn't say anything! I'd told them not to expect me before breakfast."

It crossed Jean's mind that Kim's parents didn't seem to care what Kim did. Inconvenient though it might be, she was kind of pleased that her own parents did care.

CHAPTER 12

THE cast party was forgotten in the pressure of preparing for the orchestra spring concert, scheduled for the second Sunday in April. This was the program in which Jean was playing a Mozart piano concerto, and Miss Austin was as much interested in the orchestra concert as Jean herself.

" This concerto has been arranged so that the orchestra part can be played on a second piano," she told Jean, as they were working on it. " It might be good to include in your recital in May — would you like to? I could play the second part with you."

The recital in May had become the most important event in Jean's spring program, overshadowing even the orchestra concert. Miss Austin had scheduled the recital for a week end when the Overton Scholarship Committee would be in town to hear and interview applicants for music scholarships, and she was sure they would attend. Jean was alternately excited about the program, apprehensive, and somewhat frightened by the importance of the occasion. Her teacher and her parents both told her that the only reason she was frightened was because she was not yet sure of herself.

" But you will be perfectly sure before the day arrives,"

said Miss Austin confidently. "And this orchestra program is an excellent chance for a kind of dress rehearsal for that particular number. I'll be there listening, you know."

Miss Austin was not the only one interested in the spring concert. Betsy was looking forward with great eagerness to the program. In the past week she had challenged the first chair in her own orchestra, and had won the top position for as long as she could hold it. With this new achievement she had begun again to work hard. The defeated first violinist had threatened to retake the position, and Betsy suddenly was willing to practice exercises and scales as much as her teacher asked. She looked forward not only to playing in the high school orchestra, but to being first violin there. And cocky as she was about her ability, she recognized that she had a lot of work to do before she could play the way Kim did.

The orchestra, keyed up for the event, had sold enough tickets to fill the auditorium. The reputation of the Sherwood orchestra was such that their concerts always drew a capacity audience, including many townsfolk whose children had played in former years.

The week before the concert was devoted to overtime rehearsals, and the orchestra stayed after school every night for two hours. The concerto was going beautifully, Jean felt. The piano and the instruments, under Kim's leadership, responded to each other in perfect understanding and harmony.

On Tuesday Jean waited for Kim, who wanted to speak with the director.

"But I can't excuse you," she heard Mr. Friedman say emphatically. "You've known about this date for weeks. This is the most important appearance of the orchestra in the whole year. No one can be excused."

Kim shrugged charmingly.

"I'm terribly sorry, Mr. Friedman," she said, smiling at him as if she knew he would understand. "But I've had this date since last Christmas with someone in Chicago, and I can't change it."

He looked at her sternly.

"You know, of course, that you're letting down the whole orchestra? You've led them well, and they all count on you."

"Bonnie can do it just as well as I can," Kim said generously. "She'd love the chance."

"Bonnie will be very good," the director agreed. "And perhaps the orchestra will be happier with her for the rest of the year. I'll have to drop you from the group, Kim, if you miss this concert."

Again she shrugged. "I'm sorry," she said, and she sounded as if she really was sorry. "There just isn't anything I can do about it."

Mr. Friedman's face was puzzled, as he watched her walk over to join Jean, waiting for her at the door. Jean thought, glancing from Kim to the director, that there must be some reason for this development. She would not condemn her friend until she had heard more explanation from her.

"I'll miss you," said Jean, as they walked through the long hall together to the door on the parking lot. She climbed into Kim's car, and Kim laid her violin on the back seat. "Do you really think Bonnie can do the job?"

"Sure she can," said Kim indifferently, backing the car into the driving lane.

"But what happened?" Jean asked. "You never mentioned not playing to me. I mean — is it some emergency? "

(But Kim had said she'd had the date since Christmas, and Jean began to feel chilled.)

" I'll tell you what happened — I couldn't tell Mr. Friedman all of it," Kim said. " Nicky called yesterday — you know, he almost never calls — he said he'd scheduled me for a tryout on Sunday afternoon. They're trying out a couple of parts in his play, to go into rehearsal for the road while the regulars go back to New York. If I could get a part in that show, I could go on the stage, and if I had the part, the folks wouldn't object so much."

But she had said she had had this date since Christmas, Jean thought again, feeling as if she were repeating herself.

" The best part of the whole deal," Kim went on, bubbling with enthusiasm, " is that my folks are going down to Indiana that week end. I told them I couldn't go away because of the concert — " She laughed aloud. " They'd never let me go to Chicago if they were here, and this way they'll never know the difference until they hear I'm in the show. Isn't it priceless? "

" But I didn't think they ever stopped you from going to Chicago." Jean was trying to piece together things that didn't seem to fit.

Kim gave her a mirthful sidewise look. " They didn't — until Nicky came to town. I've had lots of good reasons these past weeks — modeling, school assignments, and so on. But Sunday afternoon is hard to explain."

Jean sat silent and repelled. Kim was letting down the whole orchestra whom she had led for most of the year, without giving a thought to her responsibility to them, and the only conscience that was troubled was Jean's.

"Well," Jean said at last, "if there were any other way — Did you ask Nicky if you could possibly try out at any other time?"

"Why should I ask?" Kim demanded lightly. "It was hard enough for him to arrange this time. And what difference does it make, anyway? Bonnie will take the first chair, and nobody will ever know the difference."

Except the orchestra, and me, thought Jean. Getting out of the car at her house she said: "I suppose not. So long, Kim."

She walked up to the house, feeling as if she had suffered a real shock.

In spite of everything her mother had said about Kim during the year, in spite of the problems Kim had created, Jean had believed in her. Jean had been sure that Kim was perhaps unlucky in her timing, or disorganized in her planning, but fundamentally sincere.

She began to reason with herself, acknowledging that this business was an inexcusable piece of irresponsibility, but on the other hand, if this tryout should open the way to a stage career for Kim, the girl certainly had a right to seize an opportunity when it was offered to her. She did have a right to her own life, Jean told herself over and over. And she began to feel a little better.

The orchestra spent the next three rehearsal sessions working with Bonnie as concertmistress, and Jean told herself there was no noticeable difference. Only, in practicing the concerto, she felt again a sense of betrayal. She and Kim had understood each other's music so well she had had a feeling of belonging together when she played with Kim that seemed lacking when she played with Bonnie. The new combination was strange and untried, and

Jean felt that the performance suffered. She would never have done that to Kim, she told herself bitterly.

The concert went off very well. Jean played with unaccustomed brilliance, because she felt as if she had to make up for Kim's defection, because she knew that Scotty had attended just to hear her concerto. Jeff was there too. But it was Scotty whom Jean was thinking about as she played, wondering if he missed Kim, wondering if he thought she played as well as she had with Kim.

After the performance Jean's family, together with Scotty and Jeff, waited to congratulate her and to speak to Mr. Friedman about the fine concert.

"I'm going to be concertmistress when I'm a senior," said Betsy, nudging Jean to introduce her to Bonnie Richardson.

She said to Bonnie, when she met her: "I like the way you played that last piece, especially. I'm going to play like that when I'm in high school."

Bonnie laughed, full of happiness today. "I'm sure you will, Betsy. Just keep working and you'll do it."

"Of course, I'd have to have a better violin," said Betsy, inexorably.

"When I've got my piano," said Jean, "I personally will earn money for a better violin. How long does this go on — getting better ones, I mean?"

Betsy shrugged with an air of great sophistication. "Strads cost ten thousand dollars," she said. "I suppose someday I'd want a Strad."

Jean and Bonnie yelped together.

"When you're as good as Heifetz, you can earn your own Strad," Bonnie advised her. "Until then, you can be happy with the one you've got."

It wasn't until they had started home that Jean remembered that today was the big day for Kim, that her absence had been due to her big chance in professional theater.

"Where was Kim?" Mrs. Burnaby asked. "I thought she was the concertmistress."

"She was," said Jean, grimly. "But she told Mr. Friedman a former date would keep her from playing in this concert, and he put Bonnie in instead."

Mrs. Burnaby raised her eyebrows, but said no more. Jean knew what she was thinking, and turned the conversation away from Kim, hoping she wouldn't have to hear her mother say again that you just couldn't depend on Kim for anything, could you?

She herself didn't care if she never saw Kim again.

Something basic in their friendship had snapped this week, and today, watching Mr. Friedman direct the program he had worked on so long and so hard, watching Bonnie fill the position she had worked toward for three years and lost to Kim in the fall, watching the loyal group of orchestra members, many of whom had given up weekend trips for this program, she had faced the cold truth that there could be no friendship without confidence, and she had no confidence in Kim any longer.

Kim apparently didn't know the difference. When Jean saw her the next morning, Kim stopped by her desk and said confidentially: "That was a sensational experience yesterday. And Nicky was wonderful — simply wonderful to me."

"The orchestra program was terrific," Jean responded. "Scotty was impressed and astonished." Then she noticed Kim's dreamy expression, and realized that Kim didn't care about the orchestra at all. Abruptly, feeling as if the words were forced out of her, she said, " Did you get the part? "

Kim smiled confidently. " I'll hear next week about that," she said. " Can you come over tonight after school? "

Jean shook her head. "I've got a music lesson, and there's an extra load of homework, so I'm going to stay at school until time for the lesson."

Kim nodded and went on to her desk. Jean leaned her head on her hand and stared out of the window at the blue spring sky, with a few feathery branches moving gently across it. Kim thought they were as good friends as ever. Oh, well, Jean thought, what difference did it make after all? Kim was leaving town in June, and they'd probably never see each other again. An open break before then would be very embarrassing. Involuntarily she thought of Mrs. Ballard's words: " Take care of my little girl." Laughing, casual, teasing words: Jean knew they were not as important to the speaker as they were to her, and yet she could not escape a sense of responsibility.

She changed her mind about staying for homework and walked in to Main Street with Kim after school.

Today some of the glamour had disappeared, although Kim's dimple was as daring as ever, her smile as challenging. Jean had a feeling, as Kim talked about the tryout and the possibilities in the theater, that she was snatching blindly for excitement and sensation. Once her audacious personality had suggested brilliant possibilities. Now Jean began to suspect that the possibilities were only illusion.

But next week was spring vacation and Kim was going on a Caribbean cruise with her parents. Next week would be peaceful and quiet, and Jean looked no farther ahead than that.

CHAPTER 13

ON Thursday in vacation week Jean was scheduled to take the written examination for the Overton scholarship. Now that she was so close to the fateful day she began to worry about whether she could pass the examination or not — a question that had not entered her head before this week. She told Jeff on Sunday night that she was not going to see him all week until Saturday night. He looked first as if he thought she was being eccentric, and then as if he felt that humoring her would get him farther than argument.

"That's just fine," he said agreeably. "I'm going to be pretty busy this week myself."

She had not told him about the Overton exam, with a kind of superstition that if she talked about it she was sure to fail. She didn't even mention it to her parents, telling them only that she had to go out to the high school that day for a special meeting. Sometimes she thought it would be fun to surprise them with the scholarship, and other times she felt that she couldn't bear to have them know that she had tried and failed. Better to say nothing until it was all over.

She spent the mornings studying in her room. She practiced two hours every day after lunch, and another hour near the end of the afternoon. After supper she read or accompanied Betsy, or helped Rick with some Latin he had to make up during vacation.

Rick had taken his Latin too casually last fall during the football season, and had been paying for it ever since. Mrs. Burnaby had watched his progress through the year uneasily, aware that at no point could anyone have said with any certainty that Rick was going to pass. Rick himself kept telling her that everything was just fine. But whenever she pressed him to report the grade on his last test, it was a C– or D, and once, on a semester final, he had failed completely and had to make it up.

"Jean," she said, at the beginning of vacation, with a note of desperation in her voice, "Rick's teacher says all he has to do is learn these conjugations this week and he'll be all right. She says she's been telling him that all year, and he keeps thinking he knows them when he doesn't. Couldn't you do some drill work with him? It doesn't seem to me Latin was like this for you or Sally."

"Rick is such a busy little freshman," Jean said, grinning at him, "that he never did take time out for Latin."

"I don't know what everyone is worrying about," Rick protested. "I'm doing O.K. — I'm still in there fighting. What's all the fuss about?"

Mrs. Burnaby threw up her hands. "Fighting isn't what we want, Rick. I keep telling you, you can't pass tests by charming your teachers or kidding them. Even if they think you're the greatest personality that ever entered the door, they can't pass you if you don't know anything. Now how about those conjugations?"

"*Sum, es, est, sumus, estis, sunt*," declaimed Rick. "*Eram, eras, erat, eramus, eratis, erant*. Learned it just yesterday. Anything wrong? Anybody *know* if anything's wrong?"

"You were right as far as you went," Jean told him. "How about translating, ' You used to be '? "

He threw her a defiant glance. "We haven't had ' used to be ' yet. So there."

"Oh, yes, you have," said Jean. "That's the way you sometimes translate the imperfect. O.K., Mom. I know what he needs. We'll get at it this afternoon."

Although Rick made some perfunctory protests, Jean could tell that secretly he was reassured to feel that someone was going to see that he knew those conjugations before he returned to school. She drilled him orally, then in written forms, and after a couple of days she worked on his translations.

"You know," Rick remarked, the day she was preparing to take her own scholarship examination, "after you know what you're doing, Latin gets kind of fascinating, doesn't it? In a gruesome kind of way, I mean."

Jean felt the same kind of lift that came from mastering a difficult technical exercise on the piano. Rick was genuinely concerned now with preparing for the final examinations at the end of the year, and she knew, with a sympathetic insight, that he had always worried about them but refused to let his family know about his own uncertainty, hoping optimistically that if he pretended there was nothing wrong, the one-in-a-million chance might come his way of finding that he knew everything on the examination after all. By the end of the week he was ready to admit that he was weak in some of his vocabulary, and even to say to Jean: " Hey, how about this business back here on page 144? I never did get that straight when she talked about ablative absolute." And Jean was able to say to him before he went back to school: " You're pretty solid, Rick. Just don't let it get away from you, and I'll work with you week ends until those exams are over."

On Thursday she went out to the high school for the Overton examination, and sitting before the long, mimeographed sheet of questions and the blue book, she was unexpectedly calm and sure of herself.

She read through the questions quickly before she settled down to write the answers. Then, slowly and carefully, she began to write.

At 11:30, after three hours, she was finished. She leaned back in the desk chair and stretched, cramped after writing so long. But she felt perfectly sure that she had passed. Now she could relax and enjoy the end of vacation.

Everyone in the Burnaby house seemed busy with his own important affairs during that week, coming and going with schedules to meet, appointments to keep, lists of things to get done. But the family was a refuge for Jean, just now. She could withdraw from her personal problems for a few days and occupy herself with the family ones.

While Rick worked on Latin and bragged about how much easier algebra was than eighth-grade math had been, Jimmy pored over his Cub Scout book and badgered his mother to supervise elective achievements, so that he could earn two silver arrows. He collected half a dozen other third-grade friends between times, and organized a baseball team, announcing to his family at the end of each day that he had the best mitt of the whole team. Everyone wanted to know where he had gotten it and Jean was reminded of Jeff's interest in that mitt last September.

At that time things were so much simpler, she thought, with a pang for the pleasant past. She hadn't known Kim yet, and Jeff hadn't become too devoted. She wished passionately that things could be the way they were then. She wondered if there were any way to turn the clock back, and she knew there was none. Jeff had not called all week. Once she would have been piqued, now she was relieved, although she suspected uncomfortably that he was staying away from the telephone to prove something to her, hoping, she knew from something he had said once, that if he waited long enough maybe she would call him. Knowing how he felt about things, how much more he cared than she did, she felt guilty about him and wondered if she should call after all, just to cheer him up.

After Thursday she worked busily on the Argyle socks, and one was finished, the other half done. She was trying not to let her family see her knitting on them very often. Betsy and Jimmy were fascinated with the little cards of varicolored yarns, and she was afraid they would say something to Jeff about the socks. She didn't want him to know she was knitting them, with the idea that if she surprised him perhaps they wouldn't mean too much. They weren't going to be ready for his birthday next week, but she'd find something else for that, and give them to him for graduation.

She wished there were someone she could talk to about Jeff. Scotty would have been wonderful, and he could have told her exactly what she wanted to know. But she suspected she was beginning to care too much about Scotty herself, and the idea of talking to him about the boy who cared for her seemed disloyal.

She would have talked to Sally, but Sally was spending her vacation week in Minneapolis, visiting Bob Carlson's parents. All the younger Burnabys had been excited and prophetic when the invitation and the acceptance were announced. Mrs. Burnaby maintained a disciplined calm, but Jean suspected that beneath that calm was a jittery uncertainty: Is Bob really the right one for Sally after all? Does she love him? Is our first daughter going to get married sooner than we thought? Will she like his parents? Does she know what she's doing? And can we be sure she's right?

Jean knew that her mother, who took things calmly and let her children grow up making their own decisions and planning, within reason, their own lives, was suddenly beset with all the fears of possessive parents who were afraid of their children's mistakes. And although she tried to hide those fears, small things gave her away.

Once Jean came upon her mother peeling potatoes, the knife frozen in her hand, the potato half peeled, as she looked out of the window with a faraway question in her eyes.

"What's on your mind, Mom?" Jean asked briskly. "Worrying about your little chick in Minneapolis?"

Her mother's blush betrayed her, but she shook her head.

"I never worry," she lied valiantly. "I was just wondering about things." She dropped her hands to the counter top, and looked at Jean, begging for reassurance. "We've always liked Bob, and he seems just like one of the family. Do you think Sally — ?"

Jean grinned at her mother teasingly. "Do I think she will take him?" she asked. "Or do I think she'll make the grade with his folks?"

Her mother smiled at that, but it was a weak effort.

"Yes, on both counts," Jean said reassuringly. "Sally has been very cagey about Bob all along. She never says much or tells me anything. But I think it's all set. I just have a feeling that Bob is the right one. And I think his folks will be crazy about her. My goodness, Mother, have you lost confidence in yourself? You did a good job on Sally. She's the kind of girl other mothers like. How does Dad feel about it?"

"Dad doesn't say anything," said Mrs. Burnaby. "You know how men are. He thinks it's none of our business from here on. But how can a parent — ?"

"How can a parent ever think his child's business is none of his?" Jean teased. "You'll just have to be firm with yourself, Mother, and tell yourself that no matter how much you care you can't do a thing about it. But you don't need to worry. Sally's got good sense, and if she's in love with Bob she won't make any mistakes."

She felt closer to her mother that week than she ever had before, in the new knowledge that her mother depended on her, not only to help the younger children with their schoolwork, but for reassurance about things that only girls and mothers can really understand.

She wondered how her dad really felt about Sally's situation — whether he was upset as her mother was, and hiding it, man fashion, or whether he had put it aside as none of his business. There was no way of knowing, because Dad was not talking that week. He was writing busily from nine o'clock in the morning until suppertime, and after supper he retired again to his study to work until ten.

No one mentioned the book he had been working on for two years, the first volume of a major history of English literature. But Mrs. Burnaby cautioned the children not to disturb him, and spent her efforts during the week in keeping the younger ones too busy and occupied to wrangle or make any kind of disturbance.

On Saturday morning he left the house with a large package, about ten o'clock. When he returned he was walking with quick, springy steps, looking like someone who has just won a coveted prize.

Jean looked up from her practicing, as he paced back and forth in the living room.

" What's happened to you, Dad? Somebody leave you a legacy? "

" Practically," he said. He sat down beside her on the piano bench and poked at the keys of the piano.

" I mailed the manuscript this morning," he announced.

Jean dropped her hands in her lap and tried to think of the right thing to say. Dad was so obviously pleased and excited that she felt guilty not to know more about it.

" The English history? "

He nodded. " That key sticks, doesn't it? " he said, running a chromatic scale up and down the piano.

" Oh, they're all giving out! " said Jean. " Miss Austin wants me to practice on her piano after vacation, before my recital."

A smile was spreading irresistibly over her father's face.

" Well — " he said momentously, " that book I mailed this morning. The publishers have been asking for it — they liked the draft I showed them last summer. If they give me the kind of advance I think they'll give, we'll just order that grand piano."

" Daddy, how simply wonderful! " She jumped up and threw her arms around him. " Oh, I had no idea we could ever afford it! Look, Dad, I've got a little money. Do you need it? "

He patted her hand. " You helped out with Betsy's violin at a time when we did need it. This time I think everything is going to come along all right. I don't mind telling you " — he rubbed the back of his head as if he were easing a long strain — " I've been wanting a grand piano myself — longer than you have, probably. I thought it was one of those unnecessary luxuries, as far as I was concerned. But if your teacher thinks you need it, then it's one of the necessities we can manage." He winked at her. " Tell Miss Austin to keep you informed about Mrs. Turner. If it's a good piano, we don't want to miss it."

Jean sat dreaming before the keyboard for several minutes. Dreams did come true, then. She remembered her father had said " if." But he had been so confident — She wondered how soon they could know, how soon the piano would be in the house, how she could possibly wait. Mrs. Burnaby seemed as delighted as Jean herself about the piano. But she was more concerned at that moment with Sally's return from Minneapolis this afternoon.

Jean had forgotten everything when she heard the news about the piano. Now she began to wonder, with some of her mother's uncertainty, what Sally would have to tell them about her visit.

At four o'clock Sally and Bob walked in, arm in arm, in a self-conscious glow. Bob was carrying Sally's bag, and it seemed to Jean, waiting impatiently, that they were already apart from the family and alone together. She told herself she was imagining things. Nothing had changed. Sally and Bob had come and gone, arm in arm, for almost two years now. Why try to imagine that anything had changed?

Mrs. Burnaby greeted her daughter at the door with a calm that was deceptively casual. "Hello, honey! My, it's good to see you again! Did you have a nice week?"

And that was a foolish question, Jean thought. What could Sally say, with Bob standing right there?

"Oh, it was a heavenly!" cried Sally. She took off her hat and coat, rosy and animated, chattering rapidly as she hung up her wraps. "Minneapolis is the loveliest place — Bob has been saying so all this time — and I just loved it."

"I knew you would," Bob interposed fondly, looking at her as if he had never said it before.

Sally blushed a little. "Where's Dad?"

Dad was coming down the steps. "Hi, Sally, honey! Good to see you, Bob! How does Sherwood look, after a week away?"

Sally walked self-consciously into the living room and motioned Bob to sit down beside her on the big sofa.

"We have something to tell you," she said, her eyes very bright.

Jean froze in the doorway, waiting. Mrs. Burnaby sat down carefully in the flowered Victorian lady's chair. Mr. Burnaby chose one of his pipes and became very busy filling and lighting it. No one spoke.

"Bob and I are engaged," said Sally. "We wanted to tell you the first thing. It happened on the way home."

"Well," said Mr. Burnaby, looking up with a twinkle. "That's very interesting. In fact, that's good news, Bob. Congratulations."

"Thank you, sir," grinned Bob. "I hoped you wouldn't mind."

"We're very happy," said Mrs. Burnaby. "O Sally, I think it's just lovely!"

She went over and kissed her daughter, and, watching her, Jean knew that everything was all right, all the uncertainty had disappeared, and this after all was what she had wanted and hoped for.

Jean looked from Sally to Bob, noticing the light in Sally's eyes, the tender grin Bob threw Sally now and then, the foolish way they seemed to laugh at nothing or at everything, as if they were a unique couple who had found something no one else had ever discovered.

This was different, Jean thought, feeling as if a light had been switched on. Sally and Scotty had never seemed to belong together like this. And thank goodness for that, she thought, her lips curving suddenly.

She listened to the conversation eddying about the living room.

"You're planning to go to medical school?" she heard her father ask.

"Oh, yes," Bob replied. "And somewhere along the way, there's always the Army. We haven't got that far, yet."

"I have," said Sally, sitting up straight. "If Bob thinks I'm going to sit around for six years, he can think again. I'll be qualified to teach in two years, and when we're married —" she threw him a glance, half challenging, half appealing, "I can always teach until he's ready to practice. Everything is going to work out just fine."

Mr. Burnaby's eyes were smiling as he pulled on his pipe and looked from Bob to Sally to his wife. "They do grow up," his expression said. "After all the stress and strain, we've got another adult with us who can manage things very well for herself."

Bob stayed for dinner and the conversation went on about their present and future plans. Rick was delighted.

"Gee, I thought it would be swell to have Scotty in the family," he said tactlessly, "but I must say, Bob, I like you just as well."

Sally's face flamed, Jean stepped hard on Rick's foot, at which he yelled: "Ow, cut it out! Whatcha think you're doing?" and Bob guffawed.

"Scotty's a fine boy," he said. "I liked him the minute I met him. I even liked him after Sally told me about him. But I'm glad you'll take me instead, Rick."

Suddenly Rick recognized his *faux pas* and ducked his face, blushing bright red.

Betsy said: "I'll have time to work up a real good solo for your wedding, Sally. How'd you like something like ' Oh Promise Me ' on the violin? "

Sally laughed. "I don't know yet what we'll want, Betsy. I'll have to figure that out a couple of years from now. But if we can't fit in a violin solo, maybe you'll be a bridesmaid instead. Would you object? "

"Me a bridesmaid? " Betsy was round-eyed. "O.K. — but I could still play for you if you want me to."

"I'm sure we will," Sally sounded touched. "Just keep working, Bets. We won't need you for two years yet. Maybe the summer after I graduate."

Jimmy was staring at Bob calculatingly. "Will you

pitch me some fast ones?" he demanded. "Scotty can throw them as high as the tree out there."

Bob laughed again. "I can see I've got something to live up to," he teased his fiancée. To Jimmy he said: "I can burn them in, all right. And in the fall I'll coach some of you kids in touch football. How about it?"

Jimmy's face became worshipful, and Jean thought: What a wonderful big brother for the boys! He really is almost as nice as Scotty.

Halfway through the dishes the doorbell rang and Jeff walked in, to hear the news and congratulate Bob.

After a week's absence, Jeff seemed more like his old self tonight, casual, good-humored, light-hearted, during the early part of the evening. They went to a movie and afterward walked along the lake front on the way home. The warm spring evening was dreamy with the scent of bursting buds, and in every garden hyacinth was fragrant, and the night was starred with daffodils and narcissus.

Spring, Jean thought. Time to begin over again, time to wind up the year and do things differently. And then she remembered the old verse about the young man's fancy and wished she hadn't. Jeff's fancy was too romantic already, although tonight everything had been fine. Maybe this was the time they could both begin over.

"That's very interesting about Sally and Bob, isn't it?" Jeff remarked. "How do your folks feel about it?"

"I think they're very pleased," said Jean. "Mother was kind of tense while Sally was away — I mean, you'd get the feeling that she wasn't really sure yet whether she wanted her little bird to leave the nest or not. But she didn't say much, and then when they announced it tonight, she was really delighted — I could tell."

"Is Bob going to give Sally a ring?"

"I'll have to ask her," said Jean. "She didn't mention it tonight. She's got his pin — and while he's in college I don't think he's got any money to spare —"

"I'm saving for a ring right now," said Jeff, with a touch of complacence. Jean looked at him quickly. "When I'm ready to give you a ring," he said, half-seriously, "I'm not going to keep you waiting."

"Fine," said Jean heartily. The idea of Jeff's saving already for a ring for her gave her a painful jolt, and she wanted to get away from the subject as quickly as possible. "Did I tell you about those exams I took Thursday for Overton? I think I did all right — they were easier than I expected. But of course I shan't hear definitely until after the committee hear me play."

She had the feeling that he would have liked her to go on talking about rings, but he was willing to discuss anything she preferred.

"Is that right?" he sounded too interested. "I've been advised that the Yale exam is scheduled for two weeks from Saturday. I haven't decided whether I should give it a try or not."

"Oh, I think you should!" Jean exclaimed. "I know you could get a scholarship, Jeff. Wouldn't you be thrilled?"

And then she realized that she was betraying too much enthusiasm over his winning a scholarship to another school from her own choice, and her cheeks burned in the darkness.

"Well, if I get to Yale, I'll invite you to the prom," he said, with unexpected lightness.

They walked on home swinging hands and talking about

schools and careers and proms and prom queens, and the evening ended on a gay note.

"I always admired Yale men," Jean told him with a jesting glance, "but you'll lend a certain tone they've been lacking."

"Yale, here we come!" he announced, charging down the steps. "The old school will never be the same again! See you on the battle front!"

She closed the door, thankful that this evening had ended happily. But she wondered how long she could keep things that way.

CHAPTER 14

WHEN Kim was in town Jean felt as if she were racing on an unbanked curve. But when Kim was away for a week and life resumed the placid tempo that Jean had always known, she found herself wondering with tightening impatience what was going to happen next. Kim was the kind of person who could not be ignored, and no matter how much Jean disapproved of her activities and her principles, she was fascinated by the kind of life Kim had, the unexpected things she did, the unpredictable possibilities before her. By the time spring vacation had passed and Kim returned from her cruise a week late for the opening of school, Jean found herself waiting with passionate interest to hear what was happening.

The cruise was divine, Kim reported. She brought Jean a beautiful straw handbag from Jamaica.

" I didn't hear a word from Nicky," Kim said, " but of course we weren't in any port more than a day and a half. I had a card from Scotty, though."

" From Scotty? " Jean tried to conceal her surprise. " Did you give him your itinerary? "

" I saw him before we left — we had a date the last Friday before vacation," said Kim very casually, " and he said to be sure and write. He had a friend in Havana he wanted me to look up."

Jean digested this bit of news with an uneasy feeling of insecurity again. Did Scotty like Kim a lot or a little? She wondered if they would have a double date: Kim and Scotty, Jean and Jeff. No, she decided, she wouldn't like that at all.

"Did you ever hear from that part you tried out for?" Jean changed the subject abruptly.

Kim shook her head. "Nick dropped me a note that last week and said he was crushed to report that it went to somebody else," she said. "Oh, well, I suppose that's life." She brightened and said, with a sparkling glance: "Nicky says he'll get me another chance in a week or two. He's terribly anxious for me to be in one of his shows, and of course it's the only thing I ever really wanted to do."

"How is Nicky?" Jean wondered whether Scotty might replace Nicky in Kim's affections.

"Oh, he's just wonderful!" A dreamy look came over Kim's face, and Jean felt better. "Of course I don't see him very often — but he writes when he can. He's the only boy I ever knew that Dad makes a fuss about. I don't know what has come over him. He never even noticed my boy friends before, but whenever he thinks of Nicky, he turns purple — literally. So of course I never mention him. I don't think Dad realizes how I feel about him."

"It's probably going to come out all right," Jean said, undecided about her own position in the whole business.

Jean's own parents were outspoken in their disapproval of such of Kim's activities as they suspected. Jean felt guilty sometimes about how much she had unwittingly revealed; and other times she felt that her parents must be clairvoyant. She knew that her mother would like to break off the friendship between the two girls entirely. But as long as Kim was in Sherwood, this was difficult to do, especially since a semifriendly relationship had been established between the two families. Since Thanksgiving the Ballards had invited the senior Burnabys to have dinner with them in Chicago once, and another time to a party at which they met half a dozen celebrities.

Jean knew that her mother, with great self-control, was determined not to make an issue of the girl's friendship, since the Ballards would be leaving town so soon. She told herself now that if Scotty was interested in Kim, he would keep things under control. And although Kim didn't mention Scotty again, Jean wondered every time she saw him leave his house on Friday or Saturday evening, if he was going to see Kim.

The question gnawed unceasingly, and, without intending to, Jean slipped into the habit of walking home with Kim after school again, just to hear about what was going on in her life.

"I've got to see Nicky again," Kim announced, two weeks after her return. "I haven't talked to him for weeks. He knows he can't call me, because my parents might be there. And I can't call him — he's living in a rooming house with a very difficult landlady, and she acts simply dreadful about calling him to the phone. I tried it once, and he said maybe it would be better if I didn't. And of course I can't call him at the theater. I tried that too, and he was in the middle of rehearsal, and we both felt it was very awkward."

"That's too bad," said Jean. "But you're writing, you said."

"Letters aren't the same," said Kim. Her eyes snapped with determination, and she pressed her lips together so that her dimple went in and out. "I'll have to figure something out. I can't go downtown anymore without a lot of questions at home, and Nicky said last week that he's leaving for New York on Wednesday."

It sounded like an impasse, and Jean thought with relief that if Nicky left, perhaps everything would settle down.

Kim's determination took form on Wednesday morning.

"I'm going downtown today," she told Jean in a whisper, as they met at the lockers. "I've got it all figured out. Nicky is taking the six o'clock train for New York, and I've got to see him."

"Can you get excused?" Jean asked. This was the crisis, she thought, her heart beating fast. After today everything would be all right.

"I didn't even try," Kim said defiantly. "You know how they are about excuses: Do your parents know about this? What is your reason? Where are you going? And so on and so on — none of their business, I say. No, I'm just walking out at noon and taking the interurban to Chicago. I'll catch Nicky before the matinee. And I might just get on that New York train and go with him. All he needs to do is say the word."

She slammed her locker door shut and Jean watched her, appalled.

"What difference does it make anyway?" Kim demanded.

Through the morning Jean worried about Kim's words, and her reckless attitude. There was nothing to stop her from doing exactly what she wanted to do. Inconveniently

Mrs. Ballard's charge came to Jean's mind. She was counting on Jean to look after Kim, and Jean could not reject the responsibility, no matter how heavily it weighed.

At 11:30 she met Kim again.

"Look, Kim," she said urgently, "this is an awful mistake, this idea of leaving school. They're terribly strict about excuses. They might just toss you out, and then you wouldn't graduate."

"What difference would that make?" Kim pulled out her short spring coat and a tiny hat she had carried to school for her purpose. "I don't expect to be here anyway. I'll either be in New York or be in a play in Chicago. Don't try to stop me, Jean. This is it!"

"Well," said Jean slowly, facing the alternative she had been considering all morning. "I don't think you ought to go down alone. Do you want me to go with you?"

She was taking a reckless chance on her own school standing. But she had determined that if that was the only way to prevent Kim from taking the train to New York, her duty to her friend came before her duty to the rules of the school. She pulled some books out of her locker and took them along. As they walked down the hall toward the cafeteria where they could leave the building inconspicuously, Jean thought of calling her mother. But today her mother was attending a P.T.A. luncheon meeting, and there was no way to reach her. She wondered if she ought to call Mrs. Ballard, in spite of Kim. But Wednesday was Mrs. Ballard's day for teaching at the Art Institute. There was no more time anyway. Kim was walking out of the door.

It was a beautiful, warm sunny day, and Kim said, as they walked to the bus stop: "Doesn't it give you a thrill to run away from things on a day like this? I wish we could get just get in the car and keep on driving into the mountains and the sun."

She had left her car at home today, she told Jean, and Jean remembered, with a quiver, that if she wanted to take the New York train of course she wouldn't want the car downtown.

The sun was hot on the platform as they waited for the noon train to pull in. Jean felt conspicuous in her ankle socks and saddle shoes, beside Kim who looked sophisticated and elegant with the tiny veiled hat and gloves for the trip. Jean wondered how she was going to explain her own absence from school. Darn Kim, anyway, she thought in great annoyance. If she hadn't told Jean about this idea, Jean wouldn't be here now. The golden day was not thrilling for Jean — it only reminded her that she had broken an ironclad rule and run away from a school she liked and a student body who admired her, and for what? For something she could not even explain to anyone.

They arrived at the theater an hour before curtain time, and Jean became more uncomfortable as time passed. Kim knew where to find Nicky at the stage door, and Jean stayed close to her. Somewhat to her surprise, Kim seemed glad to have her company.

They sat in the wings of the stage, where the crew were working on sets and lights, testing drops and spots and footlights for the performance. Someone yelled, "Here's a dead one, fifth foot from the left," and someone else brought in a replacement.

Nicky was in his shirt sleeves, smoking a cigarette that looked crumpled in his fingers.

He smiled cordially at Jean and she thought, Always

176

aware of his public, dear boy! and smiled automatically back. A limp forelock hung over his eyes, and he tossed it back with a self-conscious gesture. He leaned forward, his elbows on his knees, in such a way that he had to look up at Kim from under his eyebrows, and Jean conceded that the effect was likable. Only she couldn't like him now, she thought coldly — he was just a nuisance.

"I knew you were leaving for New York tonight," said Kim. She was very casual, as if his leaving meant nothing to her at all. "Has the show got a good replacement for you?"

He sat up and shrugged charmingly. "The understudy is very good," he said, as if he were trying to be fair about it. "I'm only going to be gone for a week, anyway. My mother is going to have an operation day after tomorrow and she wants me to be with her."

"Oh, I'm sorry to hear that!" cooed Kim. "Nothing serious, I hope."

"Oh, I don't think so!" he said, dropping his cigarette on the floor and rubbing it out with his toe. "Gall bladder, she tells me, and those are not usually critical. But of course I ought to be there. My father is dead, and mother depends on me a lot. My sister is coming in from New Jersey too, but Mother will feel better if she's got a man around."

"Well, good luck," said Kim. She rose and dusted off her suit, as if she had no intention of staying longer. "I wanted to see this performance today, and as long I was down I thought I'd just say hello. Let me know how things go — I'll be seeing you."

"Swell to see you," he said heartily, standing up as the girls left. "I'll let you know when that next tryout comes off. They thought you were very good that other time, but the other girl was a professional and had a little more to offer."

Burning with anger, Jean followed Kim out to the street, feeling that she had been taken in. Nicky had never had any intention of asking Kim to go to New York with him, Jean was sure now. She had learned the hard way again that she could not rely on anything Kim said. The girl had not been lying intentionally, perhaps, but she had certainly built up a dramatic affair that didn't exist. Jean might have felt sorry for her under other circumstances: Kim was fooling herself almost as much as she had fooled Jean. But just now Jean's only reaction was furious resentment.

"Come on," Kim wheedled, "as long as we're here, we might as well see the matinee. I'll buy your ticket."

"Thanks," said Jean shortly. "I'm going home as quick as I can."

Kim glanced at her and laughed. "I'm sorry you wasted a trip," she said. "I had no idea that Nicky was coming back so soon. But I really thought you'd enjoy a trip to Chicago on a beautiful day like this anyway."

Jean turned on her heel and left for the interurban station without another word.

She arrived home around three and began at once to practice, hoping to lose herself in her music and forget about this hideous day. Her family were unsuspecting. Mrs. Burnaby came in around four, full of enthusiasm for the new program the P.T.A. had planned for the next year. Betsy reported that someone had challenged her first-chair position, and she had successfully defended it. Ricky made the freshman-sophomore baseball team, and also the track squad, and everyone congratulated him, upon which he revealed that he had also gotten a high grade on a Latin test the day before, all because of the work he had done during spring vacation. The publishers had not yet sent the check for Mr. Burnaby's advance, although the contract had been signed and sent in a week ago. Jean listened to all the details of family business avidly, but nothing seemed very important beside the fact that she had broken an important rule of the high school today and the penalties would fall on her head tomorrow.

She was through with Kim for keeps, this time. Mother had been right as usual. But how was she going to account for her absence?

She couldn't tell her mother about something that Kim had revealed to her in confidence. The first rule of friendship, even when you ended the friendship, was that confidences were sacred from adults.

She couldn't talk to Jeff about something as serious as this, not when he felt about Kim as he did, not when he felt about Jean as he did.

Nor could she talk to Scotty, who could have been helpful. If he was beginning to care for Kim, Jean felt honor-bound not to disillusion him. She wondered for a hopeful moment if she didn't owe it to Scotty as a long-time friend to warn him. But she couldn't do that. He would think Jean was jealous or something (maybe she was, she told herself wryly). Anyway, he was old enough to take care of himself, and she couldn't go around telling tales about a girl whose best friend she had been all year.

She had gotten herself into this mess without anyone's advice, and she was going to have to get herself out without help. But she was almost too depressed to study.

CHAPTER 15

ON Thursday morning Jean was sure she looked haggard and drawn. All she could see in the mirror was an unusual pallor and circles under her eyes, because she had not been able to sleep most of the night. Her stomach was fluttery, and it was difficult to choke down her breakfast, upon which her mother asked her what was the matter.

"Oh, nothing," said Jean, drinking a cup of coffee with effort. "Nothing at all, Mother. Don't worry about me. Everything is going to be all right."

Her mother buttered a piece of toast and looked at Jean shrewdly.

"I don't know why everything wouldn't be all right," she said. "But you don't look very good. Are you sure you aren't coming down with something?"

Jean wondered if that might be the answer: if she stayed home in bed for a few days perhaps they would overlook the afternoon absence. Her mother laid a hand on her forehead.

"No temperature," she said. "It's probably just the year-end pressure. Don't try to do everything, honey. Just take things a little easier."

180

"I wonder if I ought to stay home," Jean said tentatively.

"Do you feel as if you should?" her mother asked. "Would you be missing any important tests or anything? You know, with graduation so close, you don't want to miss anything that you'd have to make up."

Oh, well, Jean thought, she might as well get it over with. There was a test today in French, and another on Monday in history, a major test for which the teacher had been reviewing all week. She couldn't really afford to miss that review work. Besides, she was too jumpy and nervous to stay in bed and act really sick.

"I'm perfectly all right," she said irritably. "Don't worry. I'm not going to be sick."

Her mother looked at her and then at the breakfast she had left on her plate, and Jean remembered uneasily how clairvoyant her mother had been about other things this year.

"Gotta run to catch the bus," she said, giving her a quick kiss.

Once on her way she began to feel better. Yesterday was only a bad dream, and she could find some explanation that would satisfy everyone and yet give nothing away. No one on the bus had been aware of her absence, and everyone was talking about the wonderful program they had had in assembly yesterday morning, which Jean could talk about too. Jeff got on at his corner, but he was more concerned with why she had not walked down to meet him, and if he thought about yesterday's absence he forgot to ask about it. By the time she got to her home room, Jean had almost forgotten that she had a problem.

Kim was already in her seat, and she smiled at Jean

181

like a conspirator when Jean entered. The cloud descended again, and Jean's answering smile was half-hearted, as she sat down next to Jeff and faced the home-room teacher.

He marked the roll, as he did every morning, glancing over empty seats and wondering audibly what was wrong with Bill or Susan today.

"Jean, did you bring an excuse for yesterday afternoon?"

Jean looked down at her desk and twisted her hands, which were cold and wet with perspiration. She was aware of Jeff's attention.

"I haven't got one, Mr. Grant."

He lowered his glasses and looked at her, then replaced them and studied his attendance chart. Then he smiled cheerfully.

"Well, everyone forgets once in a while. But be sure to bring it tomorrow, or you'll have to go home for it."

He went on with the roll, accepting excuses from two others. Kim said, with an effect of consternation, "I completely forgot mine, Mr. Grant."

He looked at Kim and then again at Jean, and a cold quiver started up Jean's spine. He said thoughtfully, "Be sure to bring it tomorrow, Kim," and studied his chart again. Jean was sure he knew something was wrong, and wondered, as she had so often, how teachers could know about things like that.

She wanted to avoid Kim now, and yet they were entangled in this problem together. Jean sought Kim out at noon.

"What are you doing about an excuse, Kim?"

Kim smiled, that confident, daring grin that formerly

182

had tempted Jean to follow her lead.

"You should ask!" she said lightly. "What would I be doing? I'm writing my own. I can imitate my mother's handwriting so no one could tell the difference. Sometimes it even fools Mom! Want me to write you one?"

Jean shook her head and left her with an excuse about getting some extra help. But it was difficult to concentrate on anything for the rest of the day. Forging an excuse in her parents' name was something she could not do.

Mr. Grant asked for it on the roll call Friday morning, and Jean said, "I'm sorry, Mr. Grant, I have no excuse."

He seemed to pay little attention, marking his roll without looking up, accepting Kim's excuse when she handed it to him. But when the bell rang for the first class, he said, "Jean, will you please see me."

"Now, Mr. Grant?"

"Now."

The class filed past with curious expressions. She could hear voices buzzing with curiosity as soon as they reached the hall. She wondered what Jeff thought. In spite of their differences, his opinion was important to her.

Mr. Grant motioned her to close the door so that they would not be interrupted. Then he leaned his elbows on the desk and she sat down facing him.

"Why haven't you got an excuse, Jean?"

"Well — I guess perhaps there is no excuse for being absent that afternoon. I — I just left school at noon —"

"Did your parents know you had left?"

"No, sir. They don't know yet. I didn't want to worry them."

He smiled at that and leaned forward with friendly encouragement.

"Where did you go?"

Jean hesitated. "Well — I went down to Chicago. It was a nice day," she added lamely.

He seemed to be trying to recall the day. "Yes, it was a nice day. You mean you just felt like wandering? That doesn't seem like you, Jean." He looked at the other excuse lying on his desk. "Kim was absent the same afternoon. But her mother says she came home with a violent headache — " He watched Jean's face shrewdly, and she was careful to let nothing show. "If you can tell me this much, why not talk to your mother and get an excuse?"

"I'm sorry," Jean said desperately, "I just can't. I'd rather she didn't know about it. There is nothing more to tell — only there really was no excuse for it."

He was thoughtful for a moment, and then he said, "I think we'd better talk to your adviser, Jean."

When Miss Victor arrived ten minutes later, she asked some of the same questions over again.

"While you were in Chicago, what were you doing?"

"Nothing," Jean declared. "I just rode down — " she paused "and then rode out again. I was home by three o'clock."

Miss Victor and Mr. Grant looked at each other and alternately asked more questions.

Finally Jean burst out desperately: "But I can't tell you any more than I've told you. That's all there was to the afternoon. I just can't tell you any more."

"Well," said Mr. Grant after a long pause. "I'm sorry, Jean. This is a very serious thing. More serious than you realize, perhaps. I'm going to have to send you home to stay, unless you are willing to give us some kind of explanation."

184

"This is something I can't explain," said Jean, feeling trapped.

"Then I have no choice. I'll have to suspend you until this is cleared up. And we'll have to call your mother and tell her about this action."

Jean collected her books silently. She didn't blame Mr. Grant. He had been pretty decent about the whole thing, and he couldn't help the rules. And Miss Victor was a wonderful adviser and as helpful as anyone could be in a thing like this. She smiled wanly at both of them and departed.

When she got home, her mother met her at the door.

"What is all this nonsense, Jean? Mr. Grant says you refuse to explain an absence on Wednesday afternoon. What's going on?"

Jean felt irritated with questioning and exhausted with tension. She laid her books down and said shortly: "I was absent on Wednesday and I had no excuse. And I can't explain any more than I did." She told her mother what she had told Mr. Grant, and refused to say anything more.

Mrs. Burnaby went out in the kitchen and poured herself a cup of coffee. "Would you like a cup of coffee, Jean? It might do you good." Silently Jean accepted the coffee and sank down on the couch, stirring it thoughtfully.

"You can't stay out of school," her mother said decisively. "You'll jeopardize your graduation. Now we'll have to have the story. I know you haven't done anything wrong. But this business will have to be explained somehow."

Jean shook her head wearily. "I'm sorry, Mother, I just can't say anything more about it."

"Was Kim with you?"

Jean started at the question and looked away from her mother's searching glance. "I can't tell you anything about it," she insisted, but she knew from her mother's expression that Mrs. Burnaby knew Kim had been with her.

"Well, honey," her mother rose purposefully, "you've got yourself into some kind of jam you can't get out of. Why don't you go back to bed and get some sleep? I'm going to straighten this thing out."

With a mixture of relief and dread, Jean went to her room and tried to think what to do with the day. She couldn't sleep. She knew she couldn't study. She decided to practice until noon.

At 12:10 the telephone rang.

"Jean?" It was Kim. "I'm calling from school. What on earth happened? They're saying you're suspended."

"They sent me home because I wouldn't answer their questions," Jean said. "I'm not talking. But I think they're going to find out anyway."

"They can't find out anything if no one talks," Kim assured her cheerfully. In spite of herself Jean felt bound to secrecy more strongly than before.

She disappeared while Jimmy and Betsy came home for lunch and returned to school, feeling that she did not want to have to explain to the small fry why she was home at this unusual hour. Immediately after their departure, Mrs. Burnaby sought out Jean.

"I'm going out to school and see Kim," she said. "We're going to get to the bottom of it."

"I never said Kim was in it," Jean protested.

"You never said lots of things that I knew were happening," her mother told her. "You think you can't talk,

186

but Kim can, and she will. I'll talk to your adviser too. And Mr. Grant."

"Mother, I wish you wouldn't," Jean wailed. "It won't do any good."

"Oh, yes, it will," said Mrs. Burnaby, departing.

Jean did not know whether to be relieved or annoyed at her mother's initiative. She wondered what Kim would think, and then told herself scornfully that she didn't care in the least what Kim thought. And at that she realized that she was thankful she had a parent who knew what to do. The cloud suddenly lifted, and confidence surged in. She sat down and studied until her mother's return.

At four o'clock Mrs. Burnaby knocked on Jean's door and entered, closing it behind her.

"Well, it's all taken care of," she said. "Kim will go with you to talk to the principal on Monday, and I'll give you your excuse. All I want to know is this: Why did you feel you had to go with Kim on Wednesday?"

It was a wonderful sensation to know that there was no longer deep secrecy surrounding the affair.

"I knew — from what she said," Jean said haltingly, still not wanting to betray anything her mother might not know, "that she might do something foolish — and I thought I ought to go along and stop her."

Her mother nodded, satisfied. "I just thought as much. All right, Jean. This was not your fault. Only next time don't try to save Kim singlehanded. Let me in on it, will you?"

Jean blushed. "I knew you'd call Kim's mother — besides, you were out that noon and there wasn't time to reach you."

"I suppose not," her mother conceded. "If you could

just stay away from Kim for the next few weeks! I don't know what's wrong with her, but she's like dynamite. There's the telephone."

Jean sprang to answer it.

"Hi, Jean," Jeff's voice sounded worried. "Where were you today? I heard you were suspended. What's up?"

"Oh, I'll tell you some other time," said Jean. "It's a long story. I'll be back on Monday, so don't worry."

"Well —" he sounded undecided, "I'd come around tonight, if I didn't have this track meet tomorrow. Coach says we've got to be in bed by nine, or he'll throw us all off the team, and tomorrow is the League Championship Meet out at Clinton High. Are you coming?"

"I can't make it," said Jean. "I'd love to see you win, Jeff. I know you'll take the half-mile title. But I've got a special music lesson at two o'clock, getting ready for the recital, and Clinton's awfully far away."

"Yeah, I don't think many of the students will get there," he sounded resigned. "Well — see you tomorrow night, anyway."

She wished she didn't have to tell Jeff about the affair. Perhaps it was because she knew he would be furious at Kim, when he already disliked her, perhaps because she expected him to tell her that she was a chump, of which she had already convinced herself. She didn't want to talk to Jeff about it at all — but she felt that it would be finally and satisfactorily cleared up for her if she could just talk to Scotty.

Returning from her music lesson on Saturday afternoon at 3:30, she saw Scotty mowing his lawn. He pushed the lawn mower to a halt as she arrived and leaned on it, grinning at her cordially.

"How's your girl friend?" he asked. "The dynamo with the dimple?"

"She's getting along, I guess," said Jean. "Why don't you come over and have a cold drink, and I'll tell you all about her?"

"Don't mind if I do." He left the lawn mower where it was and followed her up on the spacious screened porch, where he let himself collapse upon the aged glider, and pushed it back and forth with one foot.

Jean told him she'd be back in one minute with the drinks, dropped her music on the piano, and flew to the kitchen.

"I was just wishing I could talk to you," she said, settling herself in the opposite corner of the glider. The drinks stood on small tables at either end, and she sipped from time to time, as she told Scotty the story.

He sat up and listened attentively.

"She said she'd been out with you a few times," Jean said, near the end. "I thought perhaps you liked her well enough to be able to give me some advice."

Scotty raised his eyebrows, took a long drink, and set the glass down carefully. "She said she'd been out with me?"

"Not that I cared about that," Jean said hastily, "I just thought, well, I thought, here's something we both need help with, and parents are difficult. All Mother can offer is to talk to Kim's mother, and I don't think that's the answer."

He looked very serious. "She asked me once to go to some meeting with her, where her father was talking about the problems of the UN, and she thought I might be interested. So I went. And she wrote from the cruise boat wanting me to send her directions for looking up a friend of mine in Havana whom I'd mentioned — so I dropped her a card to Havana with the directions. But that's all. Did she suggest that I was pursuing her with heart aflame?"

He grinned at Jean, and she blushed, realizing that that was exactly what Kim had wanted her to infer.

"No," Scotty went on, leaning back. "I think you're just a lucky little girl that she's leaving in June. That kid's born for trouble, if ever I saw one, and she'll get her friends in trouble too. My advice is to stay away from her. Keep too busy to have any time, for the next few weeks, and if she's determined to run into a crash, let her crash alone. It's not your business — no matter what her mother said. Let her mother look after her."

"I couldn't help feeling kind of responsible," Jean murmured. "She's been nice to me, and we were good friends in the beginning. She was interesting too — she showed me lots of things, like modern painting and sculpture at the Art Institute, that were exciting. I don't think she means to let people down — "

"Nobody ever plans to be irresponsible," Scotty said dryly. "But you can't help people like that. Do you still like her a lot?"

Jean shook her head. "Somehow, after she let Mr. Friedman down, along with the whole orchestra, that killed it for me. But I couldn't seem to break it off."

Scotty stood up and stretched. "Back to the beat," he said. "Thanks for the pause — and the story." He stood and looked down at her thoughtfully. "I think we ought to know each other better," he remarked. "We've got a lot of things in common. I'll drop in and see you again."

"I wish you would," Jean told him, "it helps a lot to talk to you about things." She rose and walked across the porch with him.

"Of course you've got a boy friend," Scotty reminded her, "and a steady one at that. But I guess he won't mind if you give the boy next door a cold drink in the heat of the day?"

She laughed. "We can still be neighborly," she agreed. She wondered if Kim after all might have had something to do with Scotty's interest.

CHAPTER 16

JEAN knew before Jeff arrived that he had made a new League record in the 880-yard run. Rick had gone to Clinton with the freshman track squad, and arrived home at 7:20, limp and exhausted from his own efforts in the 220 and 440 heats, in which he had come in fourth each time in a field of seven.

" Didja hear about the meet? " he demanded, stumbling in the door.

" No, how did it come out? "

" Sherwood took the 50-yard dash and the pole vault. And Jeff hung up a new record in the half mile. Good old Jeff! Boy, am I whipped! "

His mother steered him into the kitchen, where she had kept his supper, and by 8:15 when Jeff rang the bell, Rick was already asleep.

" Congratulations! " Jean greeted him. " Rick brought home the good news. We're so proud of you, Jeff! "

She planned to talk about track all evening if she could, hoping that he would have forgotten about his question on Friday night.

" Yeah, Sherwood did all right. Missed the title by about

192

six points, but we came in second." He was tired, but exhilarated with his victory.

"Are you sure you want to go to that movie?" Jean asked. "You look as if you ought to rest up. Rick was all in, when he came back."

"Rick isn't used to it yet," Jeff grinned. "This is his first season. I can take it. Sure I want to see the movie. Ready to go?"

By the time they came home from the movie at eleven o'clock he seemed almost as rested as if he hadn't run a record half mile that afternoon. They found some cold drinks in the Burnaby kitchen and sat down on the porch.

"Say, what's all this going on at school?" Jeff demanded. "I've been waiting all evening to ask you. Nobody knows anything, nobody's saying anything, but everybody's asking, Is Jean Burnaby going to be expelled? Of all people! What's the story?"

"It's nothing," Jean felt impatient at having to explain again. Between Mr. Grant, Miss Victor, her mother, and Scotty, she felt as if she had talked the story to death, and the idea of repeating it was too monotonous to face.

"I'm tired of the whole thing," she said vehemently. "I just left school Wednesday afternoon without an excuse and Mr. Grant sent me home to get one. That's all there is to it. I got the excuse and I'm going back on Monday."

"But what were you doing?" he persisted. "I suppose Kim was wrapped up in it somewhere — that troublemaker! What was your excuse?"

As usual his open dislike of Kim aroused a sense of loyalty in Jean in spite of everything. Scotty had criticized Kim, but he didn't dislike her. That had been entirely different. In the face of Jeff's annoyed hostility to the girl. Jean was not going to give him any more reason for dislike. She closed up.

"I'm not talking," she said stubbornly. "It's all been gone over and it's a closed deal. Let's just forget it."

Jeff looked puzzled and frustrated. "But gee whizz," he expostulated, "I don't see why you can't tell me. I don't talk! What's the pitch?"

"Kim's been a friend of mine," Jean said, "and I don't see any reason why I should go spreading around things that are unfavorable. As Scotty says, maybe she's born for trouble, but — "

"Scotty!" Jeff exploded. "So you told him all this big secret that you can't tell me! I think you're crazy about him, that's what I think. You're always telling me what he says about things — "

He stared at her, stricken and angry, and Jean stared back, angry in her turn.

"I don't think I'm crazy about him, as you put it," she said coldly, "but what if I do like him? I've known Scotty all my life and I like him just fine. And I expect to go on talking to him whenever I get a chance."

"I guess you will," Jeff agreed, "and go out with him when he asks you. I guess it's a kind of nuisance to be tied to a guy like me — "

"It isn't exactly a nuisance," Jean said, quiet and collected now, "but I do think it's a mistake, Jeff. I've been thinking that for a long time. I like you a lot, and I admire you. But I don't want to go steady with you."

She unfastened the pin she had worn since last September and handed it to him.

"Please don't take this all wrong, Jeff. I do want to go

194

on being friends. But I think we can be better friends if we aren't going steady — at least for a while."

He accepted the pin without saying anything and dropped it in his pocket and stood up.

"Well, I might as well go along, Jean. I'll just keep out of the way for a while. Sometimes I think Kim has been responsible for this too — even when she didn't know it."

"I'm sorry, Jeff." Jean was remorseful. She was going to cry when she got up to her room, she thought. Jeff was so nice, and she hated to hurt him like this.

He turned and grinned, with an effort.

"I'm sorry too, Jean. 'Better luck next time.'" He plunged down the steps and away.

He had quoted the words she had written in his year-book last year, when they were trying to make up after another serious quarrel. She remembered how she had felt during those months of separation and how thrilled she had been when they had come together again just before school ended. Their senior year of going together flashed across her memory, and a lump came into her throat. Carefully locking the door, she turned out lights and went up to bed.

Boys! she thought, with a deep fatigue. She wasn't going to see any boys or have any more dates for a long, long time. She wondered what Jeff would be like in school next week.

When she returned to school on Monday, she felt like a paroled criminal. Mr. Grant accepted her excuse and said quietly, "You and Kim have an appointment with Mr. Milton at 8:45, Jean."

Jean nodded. It seemed as if every person in the home room glanced at her in open or veiled curiosity, except

Jeff, who sat next to her and kept looking out the window or at Mr. Grant. Jean twisted her head a little to see what Kim was doing. Kim rolled her eyes, as if she were saying: "What on earth is all the fuss about? But we'll have to pacify them."

Then the bell rang, and when the class had left the room, Jean and Kim walked together down the hall to the principal's office.

Kim held her head high as always, and carried her shoulders arrogantly. "What difference does it all make?" she said cynically, not blaming Jean for this difficulty, but by implication blaming adults who persisted in making trouble over nothing. "As far as I'm concerned I wouldn't care if I never came back to school. We're leaving for South America the day after graduation, and a diploma doesn't mean a thing to me."

Jean, hearing her, felt again the reaction that had surprised her with its intensity when Kim announced her intention of not playing in the orchestra concert. And then she felt as if she and Kim were already miles apart. She had liked her so much, once. Now she looked forward to her leaving Sherwood. It took several minutes to walk through the long halls to the principal's office, and Jean found nothing to say in that walk.

She had had only one appointment with Mr. Milton in the years she had been attending Sherwood High School, and while she had found him very co-operative and understanding about her problem then, she had no idea what to expect from him today. He seemed a remote and lofty personality, and she dreaded facing him. Suddenly she remembered that although her excuse had been accepted, no one had said that was the end of the affair.

What if Mr. Milton decided after all that their explanations were not enough?

Her knees felt unsteady when she opened the door into his reception room, and she thought his secretary, Miss Lord, looked much too interested.

"Mr. Milton will see you in a minute," said Miss Lord, looking from one to the other alertly. "Will you sit down?"

Jean sat down and her eyes roamed restlessly across the bookshelves, where nothing looked like a distraction for a waiting period. Kim picked up an educational periodical and read with seeming interest. The inner door opened, and Jean started.

"Hello, girls, will you come in now?"

Mr. Milton was tall and bulky, with thinning gray hair and deep-set blue eyes that seemed to smile easily. He motioned the girls to chairs before his desk, sat down, and tipped back in his desk chair.

"What's the story?"

Jean glanced at Kim, feeling that this was her story and she should talk first. Kim sat forward and smiled at Mr. Milton as if he were an old friend.

"It's all kind of ridiculous," she said. "If I'd had any idea that it would make so much trouble, I would never have bothered."

"Most of us wouldn't bother making trouble," he agreed. "It's just one of those things that seem to flower out of egotism."

Kim looked startled. Then she began to describe her reasons for going to a Chicago matinee in the middle of the week without an excuse. Mr. Milton raised one hand and stopped her.

"Never mind the embroidery," he said. "We know most of the circumstances. All I want is to get it straight from you — straight, I mean, not dressed up with ex post facto reasons. If your memory is fallible, I'll refresh it from my own information. But it's your turn first."

Jean knew that he knew everything, although how he found out things like that she could not have explained. It was one of his attributes that had earned him the highest respect of the students. Evidently Kim recognized his knowledge too. With a small shrug, she told her story straightforwardly.

"But I can't see that it's anyone's business but mine," she said candidly. "The only reason I came here today was to try and straighten things out for Jean." Jean felt helplessly inept, but Mr. Milton's glance at her was reassuring.

The principal sat up straight and leaned his arms on his desk, looking at the girls.

"I think we can consider the matter closed," he said. "I might point out, Kim, that there are ethics involved here that Sherwood High School cannot approve of. However, we have had very little to do with your education up to this point, and there are only six more weeks in the school year. Our major concern must be with Jean, who is one of our own girls, and who seems to have been unintentionally involved in this. Your conduct will have to be your parents' responsibility. But it is important not to leave a shadow on Jean's record, since she is completing a high school career of very satisfactory scholarship and conduct. Thank you for clearing up this matter for us. Jean, I can understand how you were unable to defend yourself. Do you want to add anything to this discussion?"

Jean shook her head. "No, sir. I think everything is said."

"Very well, girls. As far as Jean is concerned, the matter is ended. Kim, I am sending you home until you can bring your parents in to see me. I have been unable to reach them, but I am writing your father at his office to ask him to see me at his earliest convenience. Regardless of how unimportant it may seem to you, Kim, I think he would like to have you leave here with a diploma."

They returned to the home room through the silent halls. Kim looked less confident than she had before.

"I think my mother will back me up," Kim said suddenly. "She doesn't mind my writing my own excuses — but the whole thing is such a nuisance."

It certainly had been a nuisance, Jean agreed silently, wondering why she had gotten involved in it at all. Thank goodness, she thought, with a new sense of freedom, it was no longer her business to protect Kim from the hard world, nor the world from Kim. She could ignore her from here on. And there were only six more weeks.

CHAPTER 17

IN a depressed mood Jean went home from school on Monday afternoon. It disturbed her deeply to have someone hurt or angry with her, and she could not forget Jeff's face when he had left her Saturday night, and his careful indifference today.

Monday was the day when her father's classes ended at three, and he was already home when Jean arrived. He looked up as she came in and grinned happily. Her mother was smiling proudly at him.

" Here's the piano! " he announced, waving a letter.

" No! " Jean exclaimed. All her troubles were forgotten. " What happened? How soon? Tell me all about it."

" Read her the letter," said Mrs. Burnaby.

" I don't like to brag about my general high-level success," said her father, settling down in an easy chair, " so I'll just read the letter and you can see what my editor thinks about this stupendous achievement. He liked it well enough to pay half again as much advance as he had suggested in the first place. Listen."

He read through a letter which sounded to Jean very calm, but which certainly said nice things about her father, like: " the distinction of style, combined with solid

200

scholarship," and " an approach that is at once stimulating and comprehensive," " a work that will appeal, we feel sure, to the general reading public, as well as to the class-room," " a text that will be in demand in numbers of colleges," " we foresee an excellent sale for this volume."

" Well," he said, folding the letter lovingly, " nothing like success to make a man feel good, is there, Ma? "

" I knew you'd do it," Mrs. Burnaby kissed her husband enthusiastically. " I'll bet it sells a million copies."

" I don't care about a million," he said cheerfully. " If it just sells about ten thousand a year, for the next twenty years, I'll be happy. So we'll just get that piano. How soon do you think we can have it, Jean? "

" I'll call Miss Austin this minute." Jean went to the telephone. Coming back, she reported: " She says Mrs. Turner says we can have it right away. It'll be out this week end. Mrs. Turner is delighted that we're going to take it."

" Maybe I'll begin practicing myself," said her father.

Jean laughed. "You've been threatening to practice ever since I began taking lessons."

" Well," he defended himself, " a big-shot success ought to have a hobby. Where's that book of finger exercises I used to have? "

" It fell apart," said Jean. " I'll find you one of mine. I'll sort out the music before the piano gets here and see if I can't arrange a file or something."

Her mother looked at the top of the upright, piled with disorderly heaps of sheet music and books.

" It's worth getting a new piano, just to get that music sorted out and put away."

The new piano arrived on Saturday morning. Jean was

up at nine to be sure not to miss the arrival. The old up-right had been pushed aside (it would be moved to the basement playroom), the music stacked on a cleared shelf in the bookcase, and the piano tuner was scheduled to arrive in the afternoon.

"Isn't it beautiful?" Jean demanded, circling about the living room as the movers put the piano in place. "Oh, I simply love it! Mother, isn't it wonderful? Listen to the tone."

It was larger than she had realized, rose mahogany gleaming with a fine luster. Mrs. Burnaby got a soft cloth and rubbed off a couple of fingerprints.

"Mother, I'm perfectly happy!" Jean hugged her mother and sat down at the keyboard. "I'll practice three hours a day! And let's have the recital here at our house, so I can play this piano."

She practiced happily most of the afternoon, after the tuner had gone (he had pronounced the piano a "very fine instrument"), and thought about the recital. Now she looked forward to it, two weeks from Sunday on May 24. They had been compiling a list of people to whom invitations should be sent, and she thought about Jeff as she practiced. He wasn't terribly interested in music. On the other hand, as an old friend, perhaps he should be invited anyway. And yet, as someone who was hardly speaking to her, would he be embarrassed to get an invitation that he could hardly refuse?

The question occupied her mind on Monday and Tuesday, when Jeff was still so remote that she had no chance to speak to him. On Wednesday she said, "Hi, Jeff," when she sat down in the home room, and he glanced at her oddly, and then said, "Hi, Jean," and began to study. She was still thinking about Jeff's invitation when she went home Wednesday afternoon. Scotty was coming out of his door as she turned into her walk.

"Hi!" He was so different from Jeff, she thought. Scotty was so rational and easy to get along with.

"Did you hear about the new piano?" she asked.

"I thought I heard something new over there," he grinned. "With the windows open that's quite a performance you put on."

She blushed. "I forgot it would carry so far. But come on in and see it. It's a wonderful piano."

"I'd rather hear it than see it," he said, crossing the patch of lawn between the two houses.

"You can hear it," she said.

She played one of her recital pieces for him and he listened appreciatively.

"When does this recital come off?"

"A week from Sunday," she told him. "The invitations went out today. You're getting one, of course. It'll be right here."

"I'll be here," he promised. "How's your girl friend getting along after that trouble at school?"

"She's back," Jean said. "She brought her parents the day after Mr. Milton sent her home, and she seems a little subdued. She's going to graduate all right. I don't see her except in class."

"Just as well," Scotty agreed. "Life ought to be very peaceful by summer. How's old Jeff?"

"Well — Jeff is unhappy," Jean said. She told Scotty what had happened. "And here I've got these Argyle socks that were to be a surprise for him, and now I don't know how to get back on speaking terms."

Scotty looked sympathetic and thoughtful. "Going steady is a chancy thing," he agreed. "One of those things you have to learn the hard way because you always think it's going to be different with you. I always liked Jeff — too bad it had to turn out this way."

"I always liked him too," Jean admitted. "Until he got too — emotional, I guess. If we could just get along the way we always used to, I'd like it fine."

"You could make up some excuse to call him," Scotty suggested. "He probably needs some encouragement. Why don't you call up and invite him to your recital? That would be a good reason."

"I'm still not sure he'd want to come. I keep waiting for a better reason — "

A better reason was announced on Friday. Jeff had won the Yale scholarship for which he had taken the exams a week before. Jean's first reaction was astonished delight. She remembered afterward that this would mean that Jeff would not be going to Overton, as he had talked of doing, and she felt mean to be rejoicing about that. In the home room she stood before his desk at dismissal hour and said, "Jeff, I just want you to know how delighted I am about your scholarship."

He looked up and smiled at her directly for the first time in a week. "That's swell, Jean. I'm pretty happy about it myself." He pulled himself out from the desk and walked from the room with her. "Those exams were real stinkers. I never thought I'd make it."

"Oh, I'm not surprised that you did!" Jean assured him. Then she said impulsively: "I'm having this recital that's been cooking all year a week from Sunday, at home. If you want to come, I'd love to have you there. You don't have to, if you don't like recitals. If you don't want to come, I really won't mind."

He grinned at that, amused and teasing. "I'd be a lot more excited about coming, if I thought you would mind! But if you're going to be like that about it, darned if I won't come anyway."

That was more like the old Jeff, and they both laughed.

On Sunday May 24, Jean found herself looking for Jeff, feeling as if things could not begin until she knew he was there. The piano stood at the end of the living room, the top raised, the beautiful curve of the mahogany gleaming in the late afternoon sunlight. The room was filled with rows of rented chairs facing the piano. Over the fireplace the portrait of Sally in a pink dress, aged seven, looked over the basket of greens that filled the opening. The Burnaby furniture, the flowered Victorian chair, the chintz-covered gooseneck rocker, the huge, shabby couch, had been pushed back into unobtrusive corners, where some of the guests who sought comfort as well as music had taken them with remarks about "sitting back here out of the way."

Jean, in a gown of sea-colored shantung, with a flower in her hair, waited in the sunroom, behind a screen until Miss Austin was ready to present her. Through a crack in the screen she watched the guests assembling: one hundred invitations had been sent out, and ninety acceptances received. The scholarship committee from Overton had a special place reserved for them.

At the foot of the stairs, Betsy directed guests where to leave their coats. At the living room door Jimmy handed out printed programs. Mrs. Burnaby was greeting and introducing guests and Sally was finding places for everyone. Mr. Burnaby was enjoying a last pipeful of tobacco in the sunroom with Jean.

"How does it feel, Jean? Not nervous, are you?"

She shook her head and laughed.

"Not a bit, Dad. The piano would reassure me, if nothing else did. And I can't get over how many people came for this."

He nodded and walked pensively around the sunroom looking out of the windows at his garden. In the kitchen, which connected with the sunroom, Jean could hear the caterer hired for the occasion moving quietly about preparing to serve punch and cookies after the program. She looked through the crack in the screen again. The chairs were almost filled, and Bob Carlson was helping Sally move some chairs into a better position to see the piano. There was Scotty, with his mother. And there was Jeff! So he had come.

Miss Austin came back to the sunroom.

"Ready, Jean? It's time to start. Just walk quietly out to the piano, smile at your audience — if you can — and be sure you have a handkerchief with you."

Jean sat down at the piano, and turned her head toward the audience. The room quieted, ladies broke off their conversations, Mrs. Burnaby sat down on a chair near the door, Sally and Bob tiptoed around the back and sat down. Jean looked at Jeff and smiled, and then, involuntarily she glanced at Scotty, who winked encouragingly. She raised her hands above the keyboard and began to play.

At the end of the first number the applause was enthusiastic. Jean was surprised at the feeling it gave her. She was never nervous before an audience, but this friendly, interested response made her feel for the first time that the audience cared about her as a person even more than for her music, that she was playing for her friends.

There were three groups of two to three numbers each, and between groups she left the piano for a few minutes. Behind the screen Miss Austin gave her a glass of cold water and assured her that she was playing brilliantly, that she had a fine sense of audience, and she had never realized before that Jean played better for an audience than for her teacher.

Jean thought, sitting at the piano again, that she had never felt before this creative power in playing a piece. Today she felt as if she were playing these selections for the first time, in spite of knowing them perfectly, and she enjoyed them as she never had. She told Miss Austin about it later.

"You played as if you were having a good time," her teacher told her. " I think the audience enjoyed it because they felt you were enjoying it. You know those programs where the soloist is tense and suffering over every number — you can hardly bear to listen for fear she'll stumble, and you'll suffer if she does. But you were different, Jean — you played as if you just loved to play."

Her mother's friends repeated the compliment over and over as they moved about the dining room for refreshments and conversation. At the punch bowl Miss Austin filled cups with raspberry punch and accepted graciously the friendly comments on her pupil. Sally and Bob removed the folding chairs and stacked them in the corner. Jean moved among the guests dreamy with happiness, too excited to eat or drink yet.

The guests began to leave. Miss Austin found Jean

near the piano. " I'm going to have to leave now," she said. " It was a fine recital. Congratulations. And I'm sure you won't have to worry about that scholarship. I've been talking to some of the committee who were here and they were very much impressed."

Scotty and his mother came up to Jean. Mrs. Scott was a tall, dignified lady, with whom Jean had never felt familiar, in spite of their having been neighbors for about twelve years.

" My dear," she said to Jean, " I want to tell you how glad I am that I could be here. That was a beautiful performance. George has been telling me how well you played, and I just had to come."

" Thank you," said Jean. She knew that Mrs. Scott, who always called her son George, had hardly left the house for several months because of a heart condition. " I feel complimented that you came," Jean said, glancing from Mrs. Scott to her son, who grinned teasingly. Jean smiled involuntarily and went on, " I just hope you won't get too much music when summer arrives and the windows are open."

Mrs. Scott laughed, and Jean felt that she was really very likable and neighborly. " I couldn't get too much, Jean. Someday I'll come over and ask you to play just for me."

" Please do," Jean urged. " Any time."

The Scotts moved on and someone else wanted to tell her how much she had enjoyed the program. Looking around as the guests left, Jean wondered what had happened to Jeff. And then she saw him, out in the sunroom, talking to Ricky. As she watched, he turned and came toward her.

"Nice work, kid," he said, shaking hands solemnly. "I just thought I'd wait and tell you about it when the crowd had thinned out a little."

"I'm glad you could come," Jean said. "It wouldn't have seemed like a party if you hadn't been here. As it was, I'm sure I played better on your account."

"Yeah, I'll bet!" he scoffed. But she knew that he was pleased. He looked wistful, as if he wanted to have a date with her and wasn't sure whether he ought to ask for one or not.

"Why don't you stick around?" she invited him. "If you're not going to be busy tonight, stay for supper, and we'll play badminton afterward."

"Well —" he hesitated.

"Oh, come on!" she encouraged him. "Why not? We ought to celebrate: my recital, your scholarship — anyway, I've got a surprise for you."

So he stayed, having supper with the Burnabys, chatting with Bob Carlson about college plans, advising Ricky on his track prospects versus baseball, and admiring the new piano with Jean.

"Wait a minute, right here," she commanded him, seating him on the bench. "Now don't look till I say ready."

She ran lightly up the stairs, snatched the Argyle socks out of their hiding place, and ran down again.

"Ready!"

As he turned his head she waved the socks before him.

"I thought the least you ought to get out of a year's going steady was a pair of Argyles like all the other boys," she told him.

"My heroine!" he declaimed, "I'll never forget you. Gee whiz, they're the real McCoy, aren't they?" He looked at them carefully. "You mean you knit them with your own little white hands? Well, what do you know?" He folded them tenderly and stuffed them into his pocket. Beneath the foolery Jean knew that he was touched as well as pleased, and she hoped she had done the right thing.

They played badminton in the back yard until dusk fell, and then went for a walk along the lake front. The quiet water lapped peacefully at the shore, the trees stood motionless. There was a quiet anticipation in the evening, as if all the struggle of bursting spring were ended and now the year could grow confidently and easily into summer.

Jean's own mood was in key with the evening, as if the struggle and uncertainties of the year had begun to flower into satisfaction. Beside her Jeff walked along with an ambling stride, staring at the trees and the water.

"It's hard to realize that inside of a month we'll be graduates," she said, feeling that the silence had gone on too long.

"A lot has happened this year," Jeff said. "I'll be just as glad to be out of high school. It's a tough time."

She glanced at him quickly, but his face was shadowed. She wondered if he meant that love made it a tough time.

"How's old Scotty?" Jeff asked, pulling a branch from a willow tree and switching the path as he walked. "I saw him at your house this afternoon, but I didn't get a chance to talk to him."

"He seems just fine," Jean said. "I don't see much of him. He's pretty busy at Northern, I guess." She let her voice trail off as if she were not much interested in the subject, and she thought Jeff seemed to come to attention as she did so.

But all he said was, "Maybe I was kind of jealous of him for a while this winter. But I always liked him. Remember that summer when he and Sally were going steady? That was the first year you and I were going together. Whatever happened there? I thought they were quite a team."

Jean remembered. She could think of some parallels in the two situations — Sally and Scotty, Jean and Jeff. Perhaps the same thing had happened in both cases.

"Sally never said too much about it," she said. "I think things got too serious and they found out it wasn't going to work. And then Scotty went off to school — and the next thing I knew, Bob Carlson was coming around."

"Maybe it's just as well we're going to different schools next year," Jeff reflected aloud. "We can always see each other at Christmas, I guess." He looked at her sideways, and Jean did not meet his eyes. "We oughtn't to get in each other's hair too much in a short visit like that."

She winced, but she took care not to let it show. So Jeff still cared. No one had ever told her it would be like this, when someone cared more than she did.

"It's just as well," she said. "I wouldn't want to be serious about anything but my music for a long time yet."

They walked back home and sat on the porch, and Jeff told her he was going away for the summer, to be a counselor at the boys' camp where he had been last year.

"One more month," he said. "I look forward to that camp. No problems, no decisions, just a mob of little boys to keep from drowning themselves. No girls — no dates —

say, that reminds me, we ought to have one more date before graduation. Will you go to the Senior Prom with me?"

In spite of himself, a wistfulness crept into his voice. Jean patted his hand.

"It's the only Senior Prom you're likely to go to in high school," he said, bantering with an effort. "How about it?"

She appreciated the effort. "I'd be delighted to go, Jeff. It would be the perfect ending for the year."

"O.K., then." He got up reluctantly and moved toward the steps. "Time to be going. Exams are still ahead. Take it easy, kid. If you want to celebrate some Saturday night before the prom, just give me a wink and I'll be around."

She watched him go down the street, affectionately, somehow protectively, hoping he would be happy.

Maybe he'll find some nice girl at one of those Eastern colleges, she thought, and was surprised that the thought gave her a little pang.

Then she turned into the house. In the lamplight the new piano gleamed darkly, and she walked over and caressed it with her fingers. She could hardly wait for summer to begin. Long, uncrowded days when she could work on that piano!

And all summer Scotty would be home.

ANNE EMERY was the oldest of five children, and has lived most of her life in Evanston, Illinois. She attended Northwestern University, where she received a B.A. degree, and following graduation she spent a year abroad with her family, studying French at the University of Grenoble. On her return to Evanston, she taught school for several years, where she became acquainted, in the seventh and eighth grades, with the interests of the girls for whom she now writes books.

During this period she married John D. Emery. In 1941, when her second daughter was not yet a year old, she began to write, impelled by the realization that the intention had lain dormant since her year abroad and that the time had come to get started. Earliest publication was in the church magazines, where she began with short stories for tiny tots, progressing in reader interest through nine-to-twelve stories, and finding at the teen-age level the field she liked best, from the standpoint both of story material and of reading audience. Her first book for girls was published in 1946, and since that time she has written many others, among which *Senior Year, Going Steady, Sorority*

Girl, and *Vagabond Summer* have been the most popular.

She now has a family of four girls and a boy. The oldest girl is in high school, so her high school data at first hand is accurate and timely. Two of the girls are studying violin, and Mrs. Emery's interests, after her writing, center about music (she plays the piano for her violinists), school activities (the children are in three different schools now), and civic affairs, in which her husband is very active. She still believes, after exploring the interests of young people for many years, that high school girls are the most interesting people about whom and for whom she could write.